One
Dog
Happy

The

John

Simmons

Short

Fiction

Award

University of

Iowa Press

Iowa City

*Molly
McNett*

*One
Dog
Happy*

University of Iowa Press, Iowa City 52242
www.uiowapress.org

Printed in the United States of America
The University of Iowa Press is a member of Green Press
Initiative and is committed to preserving natural resources.
Printed on acid-free paper

Library of Congress Cataloging-in-Publication Data
McNett, Molly, 1966–
   One dog happy / Molly McNett.
      p.   cm. — (The John Simmons short fiction award)
   ISBN-13: 978-1-58729-687-1 (pbk.)
   ISBN-10: 1-58729-687-x (pbk.)
   1. Young women—Fiction.   2. Girls—Fiction.   3. United
States—Social life and customs—Fiction.   I. Title.
   PS3613.C5863O54   2008
   813'.6—dc22   2008010759

08   09   10   11   12   P   5   4   3   2   1

For Dan

Contents

ACKNOWLEDGMENTS

I thank the editors of the publications in which these stories have appeared: "Catalog Sales," *New England Review* and *The Best American Nonrequired Reading 2005;* "Bactine," *Missouri Review;* "Alewives," *Black Warrior Review;* "Wishbone" ("Rumor's Gift"), *New Letters;* and "Helping" ("The Book of Signs"), *Crazyhorse.*

For their generosity in all things, I thank my parents, Mike and Judy McNett. Joe O'Malley gave me the rather extraordinary gift of sending these stories to journals for me, and a gal could never ask for a truer friend. Helpful suggestions, encouragement, and auspicious tips were offered by many fellow students and writing friends, among them Darrach Dolan, Antoine Wilson, David Koon, Pat Nelson, Cris Mazza, Amy Newman, and Blue Montakhab.

Thanks also to Holly Carver and the team at the University of Iowa Press. Connie Brothers made it possible for me to attend the Iowa Writers' Workshop with a baby in tow, and my teachers there provided inspiration and wisdom: James Alan McPherson, Marilynne Robinson, Elizabeth McCracken, and the incomparable Frank Conroy.

And as always, thanks and love to my husband, Dan, who is fun to giggle with and never complains that I'm more trouble than it's worth.

One
Dog
Happy

Catalog Sales

Our parents divorced when I was nine and my sister, Melcy, was eleven. That was the year that Melcy and I moved to town with my mom and spent weekends with my dad in our old house in the country. While we were there, he would sometimes go out to do chores or errands or something, and I used that time to snoop around. At first, I only found a few things that I'd never noticed when we lived there full-time. There was an enema two-pack in the bathroom with only one of the two left. And the bedroom closet that used to be my mom's was entirely full of Angel Soft toilet tissue, all the way up to the bar you were supposed to hang clothes on. That was funny to look at, but since my dad was a notorious cheapskate, not mysterious or anything.

Then one day I looked through his rolltop desk and found a U.S. passport. This was strange for a couple of reasons. First, it was hard to imagine my dad going to another country. His brother, Ron, had been a foreign exchange student back when they were in high school, and my dad always said, "Ron means well, but he don't have a brain in his skull." Uncle Ron had wanted to go to Europe, but he got sent to Africa instead and came back weighing a hundred thirty, which is actually not very much for a tall person. My dad would bring that up at Thanksgiving, and Uncle Ron would say, "Well, it was something different, anyway," and dad would repeat, "something different," and roll his eyes at us.

Also, there was the money. According to Melcy, it was why our parents divorced. Before the divorce, my dad used to own a farm. Afterward someone else owned it, and he cash-rented from that person. My mom used to own the Little Dancers' Studio in town, but after the divorce she just taught there, so it was kind of the same thing, except that my mom liked to spend money. My dad didn't. You wouldn't think of my dad going on vacation, unless it was a place you could camp and maybe catch your own fish.

I had the feeling if I kept snooping I'd find something else, and pretty soon I did: a phone bill, stuffed between some papers on his rolltop desk.

"Two hundred sixty-two dollars. That's a lot for long distance, right?"

Melcy was in the kitchen making frosting, which was always the first thing she did when she was unsupervised. She liked to eat it straight from the bowl.

Underneath the phone bill was a Farm and Fleet sale flyer. "Huffy Bikes for sixty-five dollars," I yelled to Melcy. "Rollerblades, forty-eight."

"That's too expensive," she said. "You can get them for forty some places."

"Which can you get for forty? The bikes?"

Under the sale flyer was a soft-cover catalog with a row of black-and-white pictures on it. It looked like a junior high yearbook. It was folded back to one page, and a few pictures were circled in red pen.

"#45902 Cherry," it said under one picture. "Age: 19. I am

pleasant friendly I enjoy cooking dancing and singing in a band. Seeking marriage with family values man and loving with responsibility."

I looked at the phone bill again. Two calls on the bill to Manila, the Philippines.

"Dad's going to the Philippines," I yelled.

Melcy ran into the room, and we started flipping through the catalog. There was more than one woman circled. Some had their hair pinned up with flowers on one side.

Melcy grabbed the magazine.

"I had it first."

"Stop, Tammy. It'll rip." I let go and read over her shoulder. Some of the descriptions said the girls liked to cook or clean house. The word "pleasant" was in two of the ads my dad had circled. I thought about that. My mom was many things, but she wasn't really pleasant. On some days it seemed to me that she argued with almost everything anyone said. The girls my dad had circled were nineteen, eighteen, and twenty-three.

"How old's Dad?" I asked.

"Forty-six." Melcy was turning the pages fast so that I could only read part of the entries. I saw a girl who looked about my age, wearing a green plaid skirt with some kind of sweatpants under it instead of tights and a tan striped top that looked like a tennis uniform. Her hair was long and tangled. She was missing a tooth in front, but her smile was wide and proud, as if she considered this a good feature. "Looking for some companion to write letters," it said.

"Wait," I said. "That one wants a pen pal." I liked the idea of a foreign pen pal. If I wrote this one, I would ask why she wore sweatpants under her skirt and why she didn't match a solid color with the plaid instead of stripes. Was it the fashion there?

"You think you can get a pen pal from the same place Dad is getting a girlfriend?"

"No," I said, though I wasn't sure why I couldn't.

We closed the rolltop desk, with the phone bill and catalog between the junk mail, the way we found it. Then we went outside to feed the horses. My mom and dad used to ride together but not anymore, so the horses just grazed all summer and got very fat.

Lately their manes always had burrs in them. We tried to throw at the same time so they wouldn't fight, but it never worked. The brown horse would follow the black from one pile to the other, pushing him away. The black horse hardly got to eat, but neither did the brown one, he was so busy defending both the piles. Melcy and I stood there watching them, thinking about our dad and the catalog and wondering exactly what to make of it.

"Maybe he wants to do something different," said Melcy.

The family Uncle Ron had stayed with in Africa ate only balls of raw dough, and they all washed with just one sponge. One of these reasons was why he got worms. After Uncle Ron got home, the father of the family kept writing letters asking Ron to send him a car. Every Christmas my dad would read Uncle Ron's Christmas cards out loud until he got to the one that said "Joyous Noel! I am still awaiting my car!" Everybody would laugh and laugh. When I first heard this I was pretty little, and I pictured Uncle Ron putting stamps over the windshield of his car and parking it on a street corner next to the out-of-town mailbox. I thought you would have to cover the whole windshield, maybe the entire car, with stamps. But he actually never sent it.

We went inside and finished the frosting and then drank some water, because eating straight frosting makes you very thirsty, and all that time we tried to think about how we could get more information about the catalog and the pictures and whether we should say anything, and Melcy decided that we should just ask my dad when he got back.

So that is what she did, just like that, and he told us: he had already gone to the Philippines. If we had done a better job of snooping, we would have seen the stamp on his passport. Then he cleared his throat and said that actually, see, the fact was that we would see her in person because she was coming here in a week. Her tourist visa would expire in three months. Sometime before that, they would get married.

"Next week?" Melcy asked. "She's coming next week?"

"Don't tell your mother about the marriage part right away," he said. "You know how she gets about things."

So when our mother picked us up that Sunday, Melcy told her about Dad and the woman and the visit, but she didn't say anything about the marriage, just like our dad had asked. It was raining and the defrost was broken on our van, and our mom kept wiping a little spot with her hand and leaning forward to see out of it, muttering "Unbelievable" in a low voice as the wipers clicked back and forth.

Then she said, "How old is she?"

"Twenty-three," I said. At the same time Melcy said, "We don't know." Then she shot me a look.

"She dresses cheap," said Melcy.

"I bet," my mom snapped.

"So do we," I whispered to Melcy. Melcy just clucked her tongue, but she knew it was true. Ever since the divorce there was a lot of economizing on everything. We didn't get an allowance anymore, and my mom drove an old car that needed a new muffler and sometimes broke down so that we had to get rides from our aunt Becky, and the piping on our couch ripped out and we just cut it off with scissors instead of buying a new couch or even a slipcover, which my dad told my mom was too expensive.

That was how their fights used to start before the divorce. She got piles of catalogs in the mail. She would show him something she wanted and he would say it was too expensive, and she'd say but look, it's the most beautiful thing. Have you ever seen a blue so bright and cheery like that, or, it's lined, it's loden, it's so well made, but he would just repeat: it's too expensive. A lot of times she bought it anyway, and he'd say she had a problem with money. Sometimes back then I would think he was just being mean to her, but lately I thought it might be true. She didn't have a Visa card since the divorce, but the UPS truck came at least once a week to our house in town. A lot of times she'd blow through her checking and have to return what she bought. Then my dad started bringing cash instead of his usual child support checks. They would sit together at the table, and he would divide the cash into envelopes for each category of spending—food, clothing, propane—and my dad would go through it with her: You see? You see? And she would nod, although usually her eyes would be glazed over or she'd be chewing on a nail or shaking a foot or something.

Once, after they had been doing this a few months, my mom took the cash from two envelopes at once and we went shopping for school clothes, but then she saw a purse she wanted to buy—she kind of collected purses—and we only had enough money left for Cokes and a Cinnabon, split between the three of us.

The next month we got lucky, and she bought us Abercrombie shirts in melon and blueberry, with bell sleeves. Then she had to go to my dad for more money before the month was over. After that, my dad took over buying clothes for Melcy and me.

What this meant was Goodwill boxes, the kind you get when they are trying to clear their stock and you get all you can cram into a box for two dollars. Let's just say that they weren't the kinds of things my mom used to get us. The actual boxes you filled up at the box sales were the ones that people had donated stuff in, and they usually said things like GARAGE SALE or JUNK on the side.

Some of the clothes were junk. They smelled like mothballs and were worn-looking or out of style, but to tell you the truth I didn't mind it. I had a best friend, Jill, and two other friends, Madeline and another Jill, and when they came over we'd try on the worst-looking things, like pink lycra tights that were pilled from the dryer and striped knit caps, the kind with the tassel down to your knees. Then we'd top it off with some protective goggles or cheater reading glasses I'd tucked in the box when my dad wasn't looking. When we looked truly obnoxious, we'd put whole packs of gum in our mouths at one time and walk to the Dollar Store and ask the clerk the price of one thing after another.

How much is this?

A dollar.

What about this one?

I'm sorry, I can't hardly understand you—

What's it cost?

Well, everything's a dollar . . .

So how much is this, then?

That was how we were, doing stupid things like that. We didn't care about what we looked like. Although one time, when my best friend, Jill, and I were standing at our bathroom mirror trying on some herbicide caps, she said, "We're not raving beauties, you know." That surprised me. Not where Jill was concerned, because her teeth stuck out in every direction, like someone had squeezed her head really hard, and she had huge octagon glasses like her mother's, only her mother's were on a chain. But when I looked at myself, my teeth and face looked normal, and nice enough.

All of this was different for Melcy. Her year was seventh grade, and that was when people divided up in a much more permanent way. Melcy and her friends—Terri, Beth, and Lisa—were the most popular group. They dressed in a very specific way, nothing like what we got from the Goodwill boxes. But since my dad had taken over, that was almost all we'd been getting. Melcy's wide-leg jeans from last year were a size too small, and when wide legs get short you can't pretend they're Capri pants or anything. When you sit down, your socks show, and sometimes part of your bare leg if you don't wear kneesocks. My dad even noticed this was happening and bought a pair of new jeans on clearance at Farm and Fleet. Melcy said she wouldn't wear those because they smelled like tires. The waist was high, too, like old women's jeans, which was the real reason she wouldn't wear them.

He got us tennis shoes at the same Farm and Fleet sale, but Melcy's said *Ladies' Walkers* on the tongue, which she said was mortifying. Whenever we left the house, she wore her stacked platforms, which were half a size too small. At the end of the day her pinkie toes would be very red and squished-looking.

When you wear jeans or shoes that are too small, you can get a pinched feeling about everything, and that's how she was to be around. She was acting different with everybody, even her own friends. She never invited them over or went bike riding or downtown with them like she used to. Still, when she was in a mood to talk, that was who she talked about. I knew Cheryl had a new dog and that Beth was using pepper polish to stop biting her nails and that Terri wanted to switch to the flute but the band director said Terri had more of a clarinet personality, and Terri's mother had read him the riot act and now Terri had a new flute, the most expensive kind. Melcy and I were not in band.

So I was surprised when Melcy said that she was not going to tell any of her friends about my dad and his new girlfriend from the Philippines. We started talking about this that same Sunday night when we were cleaning up from dinner. I was drying and

Melcy was squirting dishwashing soap right on the brush and scrubbing the plates with it, which would get you in trouble at my dad's place.

"Why would I want to? It makes him look like a pervert," Melcy said.

"Exactly," my mother agreed. She was sitting at the table with her feet up, ashing her cigarettes on a dinner plate.

I thought about the word *pervert* and how what my dad was doing was strange but not the same as being a Peeping Tom or anything, and without thinking I said, "But he is going to marry her." Melcy cupped her forehead with her palm. "Jesus," she said.

"He's going to marry her?" My mom's voice got very high when she said *marry*. Then she started to cry. We quit the dishes and sat on either side of her. Melcy lifted one of her curls out of the cigarette plate and rubbed it off with a napkin.

I didn't really think about my mom loving my dad too often. Just the weekend before, when she was dropping us off, he'd come down the sidewalk in a tight flannel shirt and black buckle boots and she'd said, "Good Lord, will you look at that?" He had gained weight since the divorce, but the truth is, he had always been kind of fat.

That didn't seem to matter to my mom anymore. It surprised me, but I understood it too. When I pictured them sitting there at our table together while they did the envelopes, or the way he would come into town to replace the dryer vent or caulk the tub, it seemed like we all had a life together, even though we didn't stay overnight in the same place.

She took a Kleenex and emptied one nostril very loudly, then switched to the other. When she was done she said, "Promise not to tell anyone at school about this, like Melcy was saying."

"Of course not," said Melcy.

I was not good at keeping secrets. Even secrets I didn't want to tell I usually ended up telling without thinking about it. Especially things that I was supposed to keep but wasn't exactly sure why I had to.

"Tammy," said Melcy.

"Tammy!" said my mom.

Of course, as soon as I promised, my mom proceeded to get on the phone and tell everyone who would listen, while Melcy and I went back to the dishes. My mom hadn't washed anything all weekend, and she used about ten glasses and coffee mugs per day because she was always pouring coffee and forgetting where she'd put it. Melcy and I kept washing, going and going, and my mom kept on talking. When all of the people she called got busy and had to go, she called a catalog company to try to return some boots she'd bought a long time ago.

"You never explicitly stated I couldn't wear them outside," she kept saying, tracing the words *explicitly stated* on a piece of scratch paper.

"When are you going to tell people?" I asked Melcy.

"Never, okay? It's embarrassing."

"You'll have to say something sometime," I said.

Melcy dropped the skillet she was washing into the sink. "Look, Tam," she said, "maybe you don't care what people think, but I do."

"I care what people think."

"No you don't. You and your friends don't take anything seriously."

Was that true? Just Friday, while we were playing Bombardment in gym, we decided to fall down when we got hit with the ball, like we were at some World War II reenactment, and that was exactly what the gym teacher had told us, that we would have to sit out until we could take things more seriously. Still, it made me mad when Melcy said it, as if we didn't matter just because we were funny.

"At least I can tell my friends things," I said. "At least we have fun."

Melcy peeled off her dishwashing gloves and whipped them into the sink, then raised the Dawn in one hand like she wanted to throw it at me, with her mouth all bunched up. Instead, she turned and slammed the bottle into the sink and then ran out of the room. The plastic cracked on the edge of the skillet and the soap oozed out of the crack, down over the skillet, and into the drain.

My mom raised her eyebrows at me and I shrugged. That was how Melcy got sometimes. For no reason she'd start yelling at you or crying, and it could happen really fast. The next time you saw her, it would be like none of it ever happened.

Which was how it was that night. After the dishes and the phone calls were finished, we got ready for bed. My mom followed us to the bathroom like she always did, to check our dental hygiene. She usually did barre work at the same time, using the bathroom counter, but not tonight. She just looked in the mirror the whole time with her eyes wide and sad, sighing and drumming her fingernails on the counter. She was a nail biter—we all were—but lately she had been growing them out, and you could see quite a bit of white on the ends. They made a strong click when she drummed them. Suddenly I felt irritated with her. "Your hands are too dry, Mom," I said. "You should use more lotion."

She sighed. "I suppose," she said, and she drew me in on one side and Melcy on the other and smooched us on the heads. "What a day, women," she said. "What a day."

That Monday they rotated our lunch hour so that mine overlapped with Melcy's by fifteen minutes. Jill and Jill had different homerooms than me and Madeline, so lunch was the first time I could tell everyone about my dad and the girl. While we waited for hot lunch, I was watching the clock, thinking about how I could give some hints and have them guess and promise not to tell by the time Melcy and her friends came down the stairs. I had to be quick. If Melcy saw my face while I was talking about it, she'd know right away. And I knew she'd tell my mom.

But Jill, the other Jill and not my best friend, was telling a long story about her mother and how they'd gotten rear-ended that weekend. Jill's mother got rear-ended about once a month, and it was always the other driver's fault. It was like she was just this unlucky person that these bad drivers followed around on purpose, like friends who try to slam you on the bumper cars or something. Anyway, Jill said her mom wanted to exchange insurance information with the pickup who rear-ended them even though there was no damage to either vehicle, and I was thinking that I'd say, when she finished, "I can't tell you what happened, but it's about my dad," when all of a sudden Madeline said, "Isn't that Melcy over there?"

There she was, about four tables over, sitting on the end of the bench with a space between her and Cheryl the size of three or four people. Melcy was facing Cheryl and Beth and Terri, but Cheryl and Beth and Terri were not facing Melcy. They were turned in the opposite direction, toward a girl I didn't recognize. The girl had a long brown coat on, and the others were listening to her talk and nodding and laughing. I wondered if this girl was new in school. She was the kind of person you would notice and know, even if she only just went to your school. Maybe it had something to do with the coat. It was tan suede with this trim around the cuffs and collar that was off-white and soft, like a collie's fur. The girl's hair was long and blonde, and she kept throwing her head back and laughing, with her knees pulled up to her chest so her hair blended with the fur trim.

Melcy was listening to this new girl too, leaning in toward all of them with her chin stuck way up and laughing when the others did. It was not her real laugh. It was too loud, and it kept going after the others stopped for a second or two. When that happened, it made it really obvious how far she was sitting from them. It was like they never made room for her in the first place.

And that wasn't the only thing that made her stick out. She was wearing the melon bell-sleeve shirt that my mom had bought her at Abercrombie, but the sleeves were about two inches short of her wrists instead of down to her knuckles like they're supposed to be. Finally she'd given in and worn her new Farm and Fleet jeans, but because the Abercrombie shirt was too small, it didn't quite come to her waist when she sat down, so you could see the label of the jeans entirely. She'd taken a black marker and crossed out the brand on the leather patch at the waist. And on her feet were those white Ladies' Walkers. Even though my dad had measured her, the Farm and Fleet jeans were short enough that you could see the gray reinforced heel of her gym sock, just above her shoe.

"I didn't know Melcy was still friends with Terri and them," said Madeline.

"She isn't," said Jill.

I felt sick to my stomach. We got to the front of the line, and I was supposed to decide on Taco Salad or Health Plate and they both looked vomitous to me, and I stood there, thinking of a comeback, like where does a person get off making comments if that person's teeth are sticking out all directions and their glasses are butt-ugly, but instead I sat my tray next to Madeline, facing Melcy and her table. Jill and Jill sat across from us.

I waited for somebody to tell me about what happened, or when, or who the other girl was. But nobody said anything. The other Jill kept talking, even though her story was finished, about her mother and the policeman and bad drivers in general, people on cell phones or eating or just sleep deprived, which was as dangerous as driving drunk.

By the time I saw Melcy again, there were other things to think about. It was the night my dad was picking up the bride at the airport. When my mom got us from school, she was wearing a new dress—red and backless. She went out to a bar with my aunt Becky and left Melcy and I to baby-sit ourselves.

We watched TV and ate caramel corn and went to bed without brushing our teeth. Then we lay there in bed, not sleeping. Not even feeling tired. It was white in the room—the white moon on our white bedspread and everything so light it felt like morning. By now my dad's bride was sitting in his car or looking around our house, maybe putting her things on the shelves of the medicine cabinet. But what had happened in the cafeteria that day was even harder for me to believe. I wanted it to be a mistake.

"I saw you at lunch," I said.

Her head turned toward me, just a little.

"Did you tell anyone?" It was not what I wanted to ask, but it came out like that anyway.

"No," she said. "Did you?"

"No."

"Good."

She put her hands on her stomach and lay still. Say something, I thought. Say it. I looked at her, the small gleam from her eyes and the white of the sheet, and her body so still I couldn't feel her breathe, and I felt a fear in my chest, as if there was someone in her place—a stranger or a ghost.

When we were smaller, sometimes I'd get scared in the dark.

Are you Melcy? I'd ask her. Or are you a woof? I'm Melcy, she'd say. Now go to sleep.

On Saturdays, our mom drove us to our dad's for the weekend. Usually she went inside to talk for a minute or at least helped us with our suitcase. This week it was different. She dropped us all the way at the end of the driveway, then drove away, spinning out on the gravel without even waiting to see if anyone was there to get us.

The door of the house opened and there was a girl, waving and smiling at us. For a minute I was confused. It seemed like the girl must be the daughter of the bride I was expecting and that this daughter had been sent before the mother. Then my dad came out and took our suitcase and we followed him back inside. There was no other person there, so it was not a daughter that I had seen. It was her.

Nineteen and eighteen and twenty-three were the ages circled in Dad's catalog, and all of those ages were very old compared to me and Melcy, while this girl didn't seem all that much older at all.

I raised my eyebrows at Melcy and she raised hers back at me. "Melcy and Tam," Dad said, touching the girl's arm, "this is Daisy."

Sometimes when you first look at someone they seem like they might be pretty, and then it is a relief to find that they bite their nails, for example. You can think, well, it's all fine, but it doesn't really count. Daisy was not like that. Everything about her was pretty. Her smile was pretty and her face was pretty and her hair was very long and very pretty.

And her clothes were pretty. I mean they really were. Not like teachers' clothes, because they sometimes have a pair of wide-leg jeans or something that's stylish, but then they button their blouses up all the way to the neck or they wear a pair of Birkenstocks with the wide-legs or they have their hair cut in a bob, so everything gets ruined. She was wearing a button-down white blouse and a lettuce-edge skirt that came just above the knee and a pair of tight brown boots with heels, a kind I had seen on a TV show once but not yet on anybody at school. And her hair was so long and black and shiny, the kind that you wanted to ask permission to touch. The whole picture she made was perfect, like girls in magazines. In that same way, it was almost too much.

You had to wonder what my dad thought about that. I could remember lots of shows I watched on TV where the man was very old or ugly and he had a wife who looked young and beautiful. It always seemed ridiculous to me, like a musical where kids are singing the adult parts and you have to just imagine what the real characters might look like. But my dad didn't seem bothered. It was like he thought he deserved it or something.

And Daisy was even prettier than my mom. My mom's body was very beautiful in a bony way, but her skin was so white that you could see veins and freckles all over it, and there were lines between her eyes when she got mad or when she concentrated on something. Daisy's skin was smooth and tan and you could see her breasts in her tight shirt, the way boys like. Wouldn't all kinds of them be trying to ask her on a date?

Then my dad announced that Daisy was making a big dinner for us, with all Filipino food, and wouldn't it be interesting? He put his hand behind Daisy's back, down toward her bottom, and she smiled up at him.

Suddenly Melcy took off and ran up the stairs, and the three of us were left standing there. Daisy looked at my dad with a worried expression, and he just shook his head, like this kind of thing happened all the time. Of course it did, but this time was different. It wasn't exactly fun for me, either. On the other hand, when someone is so pretty you can't help it: you want them to like you.

"Do you need help?" I asked Daisy. "With the cooking?"

She patted my head, and because she wasn't taller than me, she had to reach up to do it. It gave me a warm shiver.

"Nice," she said to my dad.

"She's a good girl," he nodded, "a good help."

Daisy smiled at me. "It's finished," she said. "Just wait for cooking." I realized that my hair was pulled straight back and probably looked greasy. "My mom's doing laundry," I said. "That's why I have sweats on." Smiling back at her made me feel even uglier, like the smile was the only thing I had going for me.

My dad pulled Daisy in to him and brushed his lips against the top of her head, and she giggled a little, and then I really wanted to run up the stairs too. I was not an idiot and I knew what married and engaged people did, but it just seemed crazy to me that someone like her would let an old, ugly guy touch her on the bottom or take her clothes off. My eyes started to mist up a little. I felt uncomfortable there, in the same house that used to be my house, and I wanted to go back to my mom's or get away from there.

"Do we have chores?" I asked my dad. He handed me a bag with some old bones in it, and I went out to the barn and dumped them in the old pie tin for the barn cats. It felt better to be outside, and even though it was very cold, I stood there, wasting time. The only cat that came was an old gray tom with one eye matted shut. He started in on a bone, looking up to cough and hiss at me.

"Dummy," I told him. "I'm the one who gave you that."

I got more hay for the horses, and when I was done I brought some to the cows too, just for an excuse to be outside longer. A couple of them walked over and started eating, but most of them just stared at me, too dumb to push their way in or even smell where the hay was. Cows are like that. Every time they see you, they'll stand and stare like it's the very first time they've encountered such a specimen.

By that time my hands and nose were freezing off, and I knew I'd better go inside to see if Melcy was okay. I found her upstairs, standing in my mom and dad's room. Only it didn't look like that room anymore. It was like a dressing room or something. There were clothes everywhere. New clothes. Girls' clothes, it looked like. In our size. Good clothes with their tags still on. They were on the bed, on the dresser, hanging in the closet where the toilet paper used to be. There were sweaters and twin sets and tanks and belts, black slide shoes and black boots and button-down shirts in all colors: bright orange, blue, pink, lemon yellow. Three pairs of hip-slung jeans, and one was even dirty wash. And right in the middle of the closet, hanging by itself, was a suede coat, with fur on the hem and the cuffs, just like the new girl had at school.

"Who is it for?" I asked. I suppose for a second I thought it might be for us. I had a reoccurring dream like that when I was little, only it was about dolls.

"Her," said Melcy. "Who do you think?" She stood in the middle of the braided rug in her training bra, zipping up a pair of the jeans. The hem spilled onto the floor a little, like it was supposed to, and the waist was so low that her butt crack almost showed in the back. They were perfect.

"Did she say you could?" I asked.

"Dad paid for them." She pulled a cowl-neck sweater over her head and examined herself in the mirror. Melcy's hair was long and naturally curly like my mom's, but it was blonde, which looked glamorous with the light blue of the sweater.

"Maybe she bought it herself," I said. "Just because she's from a poor country doesn't mean that she's poor. That's a generalization."

She snorted. "That explains why she married an old fat guy."

I couldn't think of a comeback. I knew what she said was true, and it made me feel stupid. I had stood downstairs looking at Daisy and my dad together, wondering why they were together, when the answer was obvious. He had more money than she did. He was fat; she was beautiful and wanted nice things. That was probably what all those girls in the catalog wanted. But how would Daisy even know what was in style anyway if she was from a poor country like that? Was it from TV? Did they have TV there?

One thing I knew for sure was that I didn't like it. I felt like one of the cows who didn't even notice that there was food around and other cows were eating first, and I got that feeling like I wanted to pick up something and smash it.

"Crap," I said.

"What is the matter with you, Tam? Try something on." Melcy took the coat off its hanger and tossed it on my lap. I lifted the tag out of the sleeve. Two hundred forty-nine ninety-five.

"I can't put this on," I said. "There's hay in my hair."

"Suit yourself."

I put the suede against my face. It was softer than anything, softer than skin. It wasn't fake, for sure. There was a deep smell to it, like rich food. And the trim was so light next to it, as light and fluffy-looking as that girl and her little laugh and her blonde hair.

Melcy took an eye pencil and a lipstick from Daisy's kit and sat next to me on the bed.

"Close your eyes." She took the pencil and drew around my lids. Then she colored in my lips in dark red and blotted them with a Kleenex. Her face had that mentholated smell from the Noxema base, and up close you could see the tiny white hairs on her face coated over in orangy brown.

"You're all set," she said. "Now try something on."

"There's tags on these," I said. "We should at least wait until the tags are off."

Melcy rummaged under some of the pants and held up a camisole set.

"No tags," she said, waving it. "Maybe she used them already, hubba hubba."

"You're weird," I said, but when I took them from her they felt very soft and silky, and the fabric was my favorite color, teal.

I stood up and pulled off my sweats and my underwear and my tee shirt and pulled the camisole over my head. It was only a little too big, and the panties fit. I went to stand at the full-length mirror, next to Melcy.

It's not like I never had makeup on before, but this time my eyes seemed like eyes from magazines, and when I half-shut them, looking sideways, letting my mouth open a little, I felt something, a hope and a strangeness. Maybe it started because there was something sexy in the outfit that made it look like I had breasts, though that was more the design of the fabric, because there were little star-bursts where the nipples were, and I was running my hands over it, moving and looking in the mirror, and the fabric was so smooth and shiny I kept going, running my hands over it.

"What's the matter? Are you in love with yourself, or what?" Melcy said.

My face felt hot. "Shut up," I said. "Are *you* in love with *yourself*? That's what I want to know."

"Good comeback."

"Melcy, Tam!" Dad yelled. "Dinner!"

I stepped out of the panties, pulled off the camisole top, and put them both in the top drawer of the dresser, and when I was done putting my sweats on, I started hanging up all the other clothes. The colored blouses. All the jeans. The sweaters. The stuff that was not on hangers I piled on top of the dresser in the closet. Then I picked up the suede coat and put it on one of my mom's padded pink silk hangers and buttoned the top button. I hung it all way in the back of the closet, so you couldn't even see it there, the way you do with a shirt you don't have money for and don't want anyone else to get.

Melcy had put her hair up and was pulling little curls out along the nape of her neck.

I shoved the slides and shoes and boots into the bottom of the closet and shut the door. Then I ran to the bathroom and scrubbed my face with Dial soap, very fast. There was a brown smudge under one eye that didn't come off all the way, but you couldn't tell unless you were very close. When I came back through the bedroom, Melcy was still standing there in the clothes, looking in the mirror.

"Hurry," I said. "What if they come up?"

"Go ahead."

I ran down by myself, and there were Dad and Daisy, sitting at the table.

"Where's your sister?" asked Dad.

"Bathroom."

Daisy served me and Dad. "This is called pants-it," said Dad, beaming.

"Pahn-seet," she corrected him. I felt embarrassed, even though I didn't know how to pronounce it either. It was clear noodles with pieces of meat and vegetable. There was also a dish of pork with pineapple rings on top of it and a sweet-smelling soup.

Then we could hear Melcy, clicking down the stairs in Daisy's new Italian slides. Click clickety click. She came in wearing Daisy's jeans and Daisy's blue sweater with the tags tucked inside the neck.

"Nice war paint, keemosabe," dad said.

Melcy sat down in the empty chair.

"Soup, Tam," said Daisy.

"Thank you," I said. I had not rinsed the soap well enough and my face felt tight.

"And soup for Melcy," she said. Daisy didn't look at Melcy when she served her. But she had noticed the outfit. She was sitting stiffly on the edge of her chair, and after she gave Melcy the soup she started blinking fast, blinking and looking away into the corner like there was dust blowing in her face.

We ate. My dad took seconds, and Daisy brought him another beer.

Melcy went to the fridge, added more ice to her lemonade, and sat down again. Dad looked right at her and kept eating. He wasn't going to notice the outfit. He ate, and he looked up with his jaw hanging open a little. His tongue was kind of big, and when he got tired or relaxed, sometimes it hung over his bottom lip and made him look slow. You could just picture him as a fat teacher that Daisy might make fun of with her popular friends at school, the same way my mom made fun of him coming down the lane.

It made you wonder if he bought my mom new things too, when he first met her. And if you thought about it, he was the one with the money problem. He had the most expensive taste of all: people who liked beautiful things.

Melcy lifted the soup to her mouth and drank it, the way we'd seen Daisy do. She had a tiny smile on her lips, and I could guess what she was thinking. There were three or four pairs of jeans to spare and even more sweaters and shoes. She could slip some things into her suitcase. Maybe there would even be enough to last the week.

The thing was, it was only partly about the clothes, and Melcy didn't get that, and that made her seem pitiful or something. It made me want to say something to hurt her.

"It won't make a difference," I said.

She stopped smiling. "What do you mean?"

I put some pineapple in my mouth. A whole ring at one time. "They won't notice," I said.

"What do you mean, Tam?" she said. "Who are you talking about?"

I felt bad then. I wanted her to yell at me or have one of her fits where she ran out of the room, but she didn't. She wasn't even looking at me, but I knew how she felt. Terrible. Like dirt. I knew, because when you have a sister, it's like what happens to her happens to you.

But it was not too late for me. I would be the right size next year, and maybe I would be friends with Daisy by then. Maybe she would let me borrow whatever I wanted. So far, though, she didn't seem very happy about the idea. I didn't blame her. If they were my clothes, I wouldn't want to lend them to anyone. Even now, when I thought about that coat hanging on our new hall tree at my mom's, or on the hook at my locker at school, I did not like the thought of returning it.

A ladybug landed on the lamp shade, fanned its tail, and drew it in again. "How do we get those damn things?" my dad said. "It's the middle of winter."

"I want more pineapple," I said. I had taken three slices of the pineapple already, and I knew I had finished it. My right eyelid was getting some sort of tic. It fluttered, and I pressed my palm over it.

"There is no pineapple, no more," Daisy said. Her voice was tired-sounding, like this was an old routine—for me to ask for what I wanted and for her to get it for me.

Bactine

It was her skin that she loved the most. It was clear, even-toned, dewy! She would stroke it, knead it, pull a pinch away from her face and let it snap back. *With Oil of Olay, I get the fine, light protection that's never greasy,* she'd whisper, then press up to the mirror with an open mouth, licking the cool glass in circles with her tongue.

She was competitive. She liked to measure things. Who was brighter, Ellen, Dad, or Mom? Which one was funnier? Who had the most talent? Let's say a rapist came to the house: who would he have sex with? Ellen, of course, Ellen, and Ellen. Because she was sarcastic, because she was "gifted," because she was not a hick like the rest of the family, because, *évidemment*, she had the best skin in the house.

She tried to prepare herself for him, because ten was too young and it would surely hurt when it happened, possibly causing infection. A vagina, when you looked up close, was kind of like an ugly wound that needed dressing. Paper towels had to be saturated with Bactine and stuck in the underwear, then pressed into place with the palm of the hand. This stung incredibly.

Just one minute more, Mrs. Bragg, are you holding up okay?

Yes, doctor . . . I suppose it is nothing compared to the pain of childbirth.

It is the burden you must bear, Mrs. Bragg.

Yes, I understand.

Lean back, please.

Like this?

Very good. Now relax.

Like this?

Here we go. You're doing fine.

It became increasingly exciting to force these sessions on herself. She dreaded and looked forward to them at the same time. As there were no locks on the doors, the sessions were best performed during the hours of three to six, while her mom was at the psychiatrist's and her dad was outside doing chores.

On the bus on the way home, she'd begin planning the treatment, whether it would involve standing and using a hand mirror, or lying supine on the countertop, underwear at the knee. It was also a time to consider what products might be involved after the procedure, to soothe and cool the area. These might include Mycatracin ointment, Pond's cold cream, and Vaseline Intensive Care Lotion for Sensitive Skin.

When her dad said they wanted to have an "important talk" with her, this was the first thing she thought of. Maybe he'd come in early from chores and spied on her, or maybe somebody had peeped in the window without the curtain. Maybe he'd gone through the garbage and discovered the wads of toilet paper with products on them. *What have you been using so much Mycatracin for?* she imagined him asking. *Don't you know it's expensive? And why are there vagina-shaped wads of toilet paper in the basket?* How would she respond? She'd just look like she didn't know what he was talking about, and if he persisted she'd say *it hurts*, or *it itches*, then put a blank look on her face.

Instead, he said, "Grandma's going to come live with us for a while to help look after you."

Ellen blinked.

"Is that okay with you, Ellen?"

"Mom looks after me," said Ellen.

"We know she does, but she's getting worried about you after school with nobody here, and I have chores to do, I can't be watching you all the time. Once in a while would be okay for you, you're old enough now, but Mommy doesn't think every day is a good idea." Dad patted Mom on the shoulder, but she didn't look up from the floor.

"I don't need anyone to baby-sit me," Ellen said. "I'm too old for that, anyhow."

"I know you are," said Dad, "but you know Mommy doesn't remember to get you up sometimes, and you have two lates already. One more and you'll get in-school suspension."

"Why don't *you* get me up?"

Dad narrowed his eyes. "You want to get up at five thirty? I don't think you do. And also there's making you lunches and things like that, which I don't have time to do and Mommy forgets."

"I make my own lunch already," said Ellen. Mom slumped into a chair and put her forehead on the table.

Ellen was bored by this display and shifted her weight from one foot to the other to show her disapproval. "Don't worry about it," she said coldly. "It's not a problem with me."

The next day, when Ellen got home from school, Grandma was sitting in the kitchen facing the front door. She had the newspaper in front of her but was sitting upright and alert, as if she'd been poised for Ellen to walk in. "Hi, Dolly," she said, "give me a kiss."

Ellen wasn't too fond of kissing, but Grandma smelled wonderful—like Lysol, only sweeter. Ellen gave her a kiss, then went to the refrigerator and poured a glass of milk. When she looked up from the counter, she was being watched. Grandma had creepy little eyes that were almost too blue, and the skin underneath them was receding a little, revealing crescents of bright pink tissue that reminded Ellen of oysters. She thought with satisfaction that Grandma's skin was so dry it was almost flaky. Compared to hers—taut and very youthful—it was real problem skin.

That afternoon precautions had to be taken, like standing with your pants down and bottom pressed into the bathroom door to make sure you weren't barged in on, since the lock didn't work too well.

I'm in a hurry today.

Lower your underwear, Mrs. Bragg.

Like this?

Now open . . . good.

Can you please hurry?

A little wider, please. . . . Certainly, this won't be a minute.

And if my husband calls, you'll keep this quiet?

Not to worry Mrs. Brag. We assure you utter discreetness.

She'd brought a plastic grocery bag into the bathroom, where she stuffed all of the toilet paper when she was finished. She then tucked the bag in the front of her pants and pulled her sweatshirt down over it, went out to the kitchen, and put it in the garbage.

"What are you discarding?" asked Grandma.

She *would* have to say it that way, thought Ellen. *Discarding.* "Je vide la poubelle," she said smugly and proceeded to the living room to get another wastebasket.

"Whatsit?" Grandma yelled from the kitchen.

"And now if you'll excuse me," Ellen continued, dumping the living room wastebasket into the kitchen one with a flourish, "I need to do some homework." And she took a pack of Juicy Fruit and went back to her mom and dad's room to go sleuthing. She unwrapped one piece of gum and put it in her mouth, then opened her mother's underwear drawer and rummaged to the bottom, where there was a sex book with drawings in it and a tube of spermicidal jelly. This was the same old stuff, and after lingering on the one where the woman was face down on an ottoman with the man standing behind her, the flavor had run out of the first stick, so she put another one in and moved on to her dad's dresser. This was not promising at first: only bandannas and jockey shorts, which were all navy or white. Below these she discovered a bill for her mother's psychiatrist, for which she treated herself to more gum, and a pile of notes from parents of Dad's students at school. There was nothing very interesting here, though she knew he had some real problem kids, with sex molestations or divorces or things like that. Abnormals. But it seemed like he only saved the notes with bad grammar, like "Please excuse Dave as he ain't felling well" or "Your a good teacher and one whos a farmer too so youl know Kenny had to hep with hay, thats why he was absint on Monday & Tuesday. We had good waether for it dint we." Ellen thought it was weird that Dad saved notes with *ain't* on them, because she'd heard him use it himself when he was with other farmers. At the bottom of the note pile were five uneventful letters regarding a student named Kookie, which she guessed he'd saved just because Kookie was such a stupid name. She wadded up her tasteless gum in one of them and put a fresh stick in. After this she went into the walk-in closet and rummaged around for any presents that might be hidden underneath the bathrobe section.

"She chews an awful lot of gum," Grandma announced at dinner that night.

"Who's that?" said Dad, looking over at Mom. Ellen noticed that Mom wasn't eating, just pushing the chop suey from one side of the plate to the other with her fork.

"She does," said Grandma, then jerked her chin toward Ellen. "I saw her put nearly a whole pack in her mouth."

"I did *not* put a whole pack in there," Ellen said. She felt her eyelid twitching.

"That's a lot of gum, girl," Dad laughed. "You'll have a jaw like a halfback." He looked over at Mom and chuckled again, inviting her to join in on the joke. "We'll have to stop buying ten-packs, huh, Mom?"

Mom was always getting caught like this in the middle of a conversation that she hadn't been paying attention to. She shrugged without looking at any of them, as if she'd been listening but had no opinion.

Ellen looked at Grandma. Her creepy eyes had narrowed, her lips pursed together in a tight line. She turned to Dad, who had his hand around his water glass and was staring down at his plate.

"Does she know what's going on?" she asked.

"You were listening, Mom," Ellen said. "What did we say?"

Grandma made a clucking noise and stood up. She cleared Dad's empty plate from in front of him, took a serving dish in the other hand, and dropped them in the sink with a clang. The longer Mom remained silent, the more horrified Ellen felt.

"Come on, Mom," she said, in a squeaky voice, "You know what we said. What did we say?"

"That's it, then," said Dad, putting his hand over Ellen's. His skin felt fishy, or clammy, whatever the word was for cold and sweaty at the same time. She pulled her hand away and put it in her lap.

"Their nerves at this age are something else," Dad told Grandma. "I try to tell her it will get better later. But you know . . . teenage girls . . . preteen I guess it is. She's ten, but at this age, especially, it's as if they have no . . . padding around the nerves. Just raw nerves. Nothing but nerves, nothing to . . . temper the nerves." He sighed. "I could've put that better, but you know what I'm saying."

Dad had big bags under his eyes, which could easily have been prevented with cucumbers or any combination of wet and cold compresses. You didn't have to put a lot of time into it to look your best every day. And Dad wasn't bad compared to Mom, who didn't even bother to tuck her shirt in and wore the same navy sweatpants every day.

If a rapist came to the house and Ellen was gone, then who would he pick? Mom or Grandma? It was a tough call. Both were really too old. Still, Grandma's standards were much higher than Mom's. She was old, but she was pulled together, wearing the latest in tasteful fashions for women of her age, including wool blazers or tee shirts that said BEAUTIFUL PEOPLE in the corner. Ellen wondered who the beautiful people were. By wearing the shirt, were you saying that you *were* one or that you wore the same kind of shirt they did? Was there a limit on how many people could buy them, like an exclusive club?

You look beautiful, Mrs. Bragg. Have you changed your hairstyle?

Doctor, I'm not sure if it's appropriate for you to—

Undress.

Excuse me?

You heard me. Please pull down your underwear and walk toward me.

If you say so . . . but be quick.
We assure you utter efficiency.

When Ellen visited Grandma's house in the suburbs, there were rules to follow. Bedtime, for example, had always been at ten o'clock, so Grandma didn't see why ten o'clock wouldn't work here. Staying up late was why Ellen had overslept in the first place. Hadn't they thought of that? The beds should also be made every morning, why not? Grandma would make Dad's for him if he wanted, but Ellen needed to be responsible for her own. Sheets would be changed once a week; she'd just checked them and they seemed sandy, like they hadn't been washed since summer vacation! And what about some chores for Ellen? Dad agreed that it wouldn't be a bad idea. She could even help Dad with some farm work. The fresh air would be good for her.

On Saturday, Ellen went to the Farm and Fleet with Dad and bought steel-toed boots and some overalls. She insisted on corduroy, which Dad said was totally impractical but it was up to her. "I'm tickled to have a helper," he beamed at her. Ellen wrinkled her nose at him, but she felt excited about it too. Dad had never let her help before. He'd always said farm work was really boys' stuff, because you needed to be tough. Even if that was true, Ellen thought it was unfair to generalize if you didn't know from personal experience. Dad had only had a boy once, and the boy had died before Ellen was even born. Even if Dad had taken him on the tractor, he'd never helped with chores, she was sure of that.

From time to time Ellen found pictures of the boy in the underwear drawer. He had been chubby, with curly hair that was so blond it was almost white. If he had lived he would have been thirteen now. She tried to think about what he would look like, and sometimes she could even get herself to cry a little about him, but not without squinting and then crossing her eyes slightly to help it along. If she'd had a brother to compete with, maybe she would have turned out better, not so bratty and self-absorbed. Still, she knew it was a sign of maturity simply to be able to observe her own selfishness. *Je m'aime!* she'd chant, while distributing a strip of blue gel onto her toothbrush, *Je m'intéresse*, turning to the mirror with a foamy smile. *Me amo*, spit and rinse, *Me quiero!*

On her first day of chores, Dad filled the hayrack with bales, and Ellen sat behind him on the tractor. "Look," he said, "these are the gears. When I want to drive faster, I put it in rabbit." There were pictures of one, two, then three rabbits, and the same series with turtles on the other side of the gearshift.

"Can I drive?" she asked.

"Not yet. You go in back. When we get to the cows, I'll put her in turtle and you push a bale off the wagon every few feet or so."

When they reached the pasture, Ellen stood on the hayrack. When Dad yelled go, she pushed a bale off the edge, and it fell to the ground. Soon the whole herd of cows was following them. Ellen was breathing hard after a few minutes, and the wind stung her cheeks. By the time they were finished, they were on the top of the hill, and Ellen could look down on the serpentine of bales they had spread, each with two or three cows munching content-edly around it. "They got a nice look to 'em, huh?" Dad yelled back to her from the tractor.

Ellen sat on the hayrack as Dad drove her home, watching her legs swing from the edge. Maybe she could be a farm girl. It was good, important work to feed something else, to make it live. And she looked cute in her outfit too. Tomorrow she thought she might braid her hair or put it in two pigtails with a bandanna tied around each one.

After chores, she made lemon squares and a loaf of wheat bread, which gave her terrible gas because she ate some of the dough while it was rising. But the whole house smelled delicious, like sugar and cleaning products.

Dad looked genuinely pleased when he came inside for dinner.

"You did great, honey! All this and a real cook, too! And a real helper. You're a big help to all of us, isn't she, Mom?"

"Mmm," said Mom. Mom was eating stew from her coffee cup. It was not dinnertime yet, but Dad did not notice it.

"The house looks better already, " he beamed.

"I haven't started on the house yet," said Grandma.

"On the house?" Mom asked, looking up from her mug.

"Oh, yes, of course. It's filthy. Above the stove for example. I don't think people are cleaning it." Grandma was smiling, but there was an edge to her voice that gave Ellen a chill.

"And that bathroom is a disaster, Stuart. People are leaving deo-drent, tweezers, Band-Aids, everything, all on the counter."

She looked at Ellen. "And globs of toothpaste that people don't bother to wipe up, which have hair stuck in them."

"Mmm," said Dad, nodding.

"I counted nearly twenty toothbrushes in the cup in there," she continued. "Who owns them? Are you all taking new ones without discarding the old, or do you just forget which toothbrush is yours? I have to consider throwing them *all* out."

Mom looked very sad then. And even though Grandma had said all of this without really looking at Mom, it seemed like every time she said *people* she was not really talking about Dad or Ellen at all.

The next day Ellen wore braids in her hair and a cap that said DeKalb Seed Corn. As they approached the pasture from the hill, she could see the herd gathered around a lone cow, who was standing in the middle of the creek. One of the herd butted the cow with its head. She stumbled, fell, and struggled to her feet again.

"What're they doing?" Ellen yelled to Dad over the noise of the tractor.

"She's lame," he said, pulling into the three-rabbits gear. "Boss!" he called out, "Here, Boss!"

"What happened to her?"

"She got mounted too hard."

Ellen thought about that for a second.

Dad's eyes were on the cow, who was limping toward the bank. Another cow kicked her in the hind leg from the side, and she lurched forward into the water.

"Boss!" Dad yelled again. "Co, Boss!"

"Why are you yelling at her?" Ellen asked.

"I'm yelling at *them*."

"Oh." Ellen wanted to yell at them too, but she felt silly saying "Boss," it was so farmery and she didn't know what it meant.

One of the herd turned and started toward the hay wagon. Another followed.

Ellen poked Dad in the shoulder. "What are they so mad for?" she asked.

"What?"

"Why were they attacking her?" she yelled.

"She's lame," dad yelled back. "That's what they do."

Ellen got on the back of the wagon and quickly began pushing the bales off the edge. Maybe the hay would distract the cows from attacking, and maybe if she didn't drop it fast enough, they would return to the lame cow again. She found that she had the strength to pick the smaller bales up from the bed of the wagon and pitch them off of the edge.

When all the bales were down, Ellen followed Dad to the lame cow, who was lying on the bank of the creek. As they approached, the cow threw her head back and struggled to get up. Her knee buckled and she fell again. Dad leaned into her and slapped her flank. "Get up," he said, "go on, now."

But the cow struggled only slightly, then sank to the grass.

"Well," Dad said, standing up, "we have to drag her."

Ellen looked into the eyes of the cow. They were dark and wet, with long lashes that made her seem gentle and deerlike. Ellen looked right into them, and the cow stared back. *It's okay, cow. It will be okay*, she thought. Dad unpinned the hay wagon from the tractor and tied one end of his rope around the cow's forelegs. The other end he knotted to the tractor hitch.

They dragged the cow across the pasture toward the house. Ellen stood behind the tractor seat, watching the cow move across the ground, bones and flesh spanking against the ground until the cow threw her neck back and brayed in octaves, like a donkey.

"Dad! It's hurting her!" Ellen yelled, but Dad didn't look back or respond. When they reached the gate, he untied the cow from the tractor and swung the gate shut behind her. The cow heaved, rolled onto her back, and fell to her other side.

"She lost a lot of hide," Dad said.

Ellen jumped down and ran to the cow. All over her side, bright pink patches of skin shone where her coat had ripped off.

She started to cry. "You hurt her!" she screamed at Dad. The cow had stopped bellowing, and her eyes were glazed over. Foam ran from her mouth, and her big belly rose and fell with sharp breaths.

"I told you," Dad said evenly, not looking at Ellen, "They'd kill her otherwise."

"Yes, but couldn't you pick her up?"

He gave a short laugh. "You think I could pick her up? You think you and me *together* could pick her up?"

She sniffed and wiped her nose on her sleeve. Dad was usually so nice about everything that it was almost annoying. And now here he was being about as mean as anyone could be and laughing about it. She wanted him to say something comforting: the cow couldn't feel pain like humans did, it would be healed in the morning, they could bring it some medicine.

Instead, he clapped his hands. "Hop on the tractor. We'll pick the wagon up tomorrow."

Ellen stood there. "What are you going to do with her?" she asked. "Shouldn't she be inside?"

"How would I get her to the barn, smarty-pants?" Dad asked, pointing to the road. "You want to see what she looks like after I drag her over gravel?"

Ellen's face felt hot. "But you can't just leave her here."

"I'll have the rendering works pick her up tomorrow."

"Isn't that just a butcher?" whispered Ellen.

"She can't calve anymore with that leg," said Dad.

"But you said you were *saving* her," Ellen said. Her nose began to drip.

"I said they would kill her otherwise." Dad handed her the bandanna from his pocket.

"I don't want it," Ellen said, walking behind the cow. "Can't I feed her until she's better?"

"She'd probably die anyway, Ellen," Dad said. "And I can't get anything for her if she's already dead." He shoved the bandanna back in his pocket and climbed on the tractor.

"But it's not her *fault* that's she's lame." She couldn't control her voice now. It was high and whiny, and she knew she would cry again if she said any more.

Dad pointed for Ellen to climb up behind him. "This is exactly what I meant about farm work," he muttered. "If I said it once, I said it a thousand times."

When they got to the house, Ellen walked inside, sat down at the table, and began to cry. She cried without thinking about it and without trying to, without wondering, the way she usually did, if it sounded natural.

She felt a hand on her shoulder.

"I've drawn you a bath," Grandma said. "Go calm yourself down."

The bathroom was clean, the counter uncluttered and shiny, and the air moist, smelling of strawberries. Ellen undressed in a stupor, lowered her body into the water, and lay quietly, listening to her breath. Dad was talking with Grandma in the hall.

You spoiled her, Stuart.

She was helping me fine. She's just sensitive, that's all.

If you're not careful she'll follow right after her mother.

Hers is a physical problem, Evy.

She'd get better if she put her mind to it.

Then there was only the crackle of bubbles dying away. Ellen lifted a pruned hand from the water and studied it.

Is anything the matter, Mrs. Bragg?

Why do you ask?

You seem upset—very genuinely upset

I lost a friend, you might say.

Tragedy strikes us all, Mrs. Bragg. It is the way we react which displays our character.

Is that true?

Yes. Please open your legs. My, you are very warm in this area today.

I've had a bath.

After the session was finished, Ellen went to her room and slept. When she opened her eyes, she didn't know what time it was or if they'd had dinner yet. Her head felt foggy. She walked down the hall to the kitchen.

The room was dark, but the little light was on just above the stove, and Mom stood, leaning forward against the kitchen island with her stomach. Ellen thought she could hear a hissing sound coming from her, as if she had been punctured.

It's okay, it's okay, it's okay . . .

It was embarrassing. It was like a bad taste in her mouth. She switched on the light.

"Mom," she said, "are you all right?"

Mom gave a little laugh. "You scared me," she said, sitting down at the kitchen island.

Ellen sat next to her under the yellow light of the kitchen lamp.

There was a clean smell to the kitchen now. It smelled different than it used to, when there was always the leftover, greasy smell of grilled hamburgers. She tried to think of something to say, but it was hard to say anything when Mom was sad, because what you said never changed anything.

Mom's eyes in the window were wide and helpless. They seemed to be asking for something, and Ellen thought to herself that Mom's eyes had been asking for something for as long as she could remember, and that it was unforgivable, and that it was disgusting, and that she would not do that to her children or to anyone else, ever—that she would handle things, whatever they were, better than that.

She would not act like a baby around them again. Not around Grandma, and not around Dad, especially. She understood how it worked. The healthy cows had been disgusted with the lame cow, but the lame cow had not been blameless. If it had put all its effort in, it might've gotten up, no matter how its leg hurt. Now when she pictured the animal, she saw immediately the mucus and froth escaping its mouth, its big fat belly. And the way she'd blubbered about it was the worst of all. *Pull yourself together,* she thought, *idiot.*

"Mom," she said, "I'll make you some tea." And Mom looked up—gratefully, Ellen thought—and sighed. Ellen put the kettle on, poured milk and sugar in a cup, and sat down to wait for the whistle to blow. *Get over it.* She felt herself drifting to a new place, all by herself. Far from the kitchen island, beyond pity. She would do her job. She imagined the tea would taste sweet and good to Mom, that it would calm her, comfort her, take her mind off things.

One Dog Happy

In the middle of a heat wave, in the middle of August, in the board-flat middle of the state of Illinois, in a college town bordered on one side by the tract housing of young families and on the other by the stinky fields and farm animals of the university's ag department, the minister was giving orders. He gave orders easily, because he was used to it. People did things for him; they seemed to want to.

The minister was taking his wife and five children on vacation. There were plants to water, a litter box to empty, mail to take in, and so on. He was rattling off a list for their house sitter, a member of the church whom the children called Mr. Bob.

Mr. Bob would be in charge of everything except the family's new dog, said the minister. The dog was "very strong" and liable to pull away when on the leash; in fact, in the three weeks since they'd gotten it from the pound, it had already run away from one of the children.

"Yes," Mr. Bob replied. "You called me to help that morning, and by the time I got dressed and got over here, someone had caught it already."

"Oh, that's right," said the minister, though he did not look sheepish or sorry. "So you remember, about the pulling off the leash."

The minister explained to Mr. Bob that he had decided to pay a young man to walk the dog daily, an army private who'd just returned from Iraq. The private's father was also an elder in the church.

"A dog walker," said Mr. Bob testily. "What's the going rate for that, anyway?"

"I don't remember," said the minister.

The minister's son looked up from his Game Boy. "I thought you said a hundred bucks."

"A hundred bucks," said Mr. Bob under his breath.

Mr. Bob had always lived in the college town but since his retirement had been feeling especially sensitive to the youthful bias of the place. Half of any church congregation was in college or graduate school or had recently finished both, as the minister had. Next to them, Mr. Bob seemed old and feeble, though he was only seventy and sharper, he thought, than many people ten years younger than he. It was true that his eyes were light sensitive, and the black wraparound sunglasses he wore often gave people the impression that he couldn't see at all. And maybe he appeared off-balance somehow, as his legs were very thin, yet he had gained quite a bit of weight in the midsection, which was why Baby George, the minister's youngest child, had taken to calling him Humpy Dumpy. The other children had tried it too and had been reprimanded soundly. But Baby George was allowed to say it whenever he pleased. "My hands do shake," Mr. Bob told the minister, "but it's only my new diuretic."

"Oh no, Mr. Bob," said the minister's wife kindly. "My hands are always shaking too, especially if I have coffee. I never would have noticed it."

"Beagles are notorious for getting lost," said the minister. "They follow the scent to the exclusion of everything else."

Mr. Bob had tried not to seem humiliated by any of this, but suddenly his irritation got the better of him, and he said in a low voice, "What kind of dog is that, then? Why would anyone want one?"

"What's that?" asked the minister.

"He thaid why would anyone want one," said the minister's beautiful wife, smiling and nodding at Mr. Bob with her eyebrows raised, as if he were a child who'd said something very clever. She had a lisp and very long, shiny black hair that always smelled as if she'd just washed it.

The minister was no match for her, but he was tall, and he carried himself as if being tall were enough. He stood erect; he plopped himself down and sat with his knees spread wide; he took up room. He didn't worry about his bowed legs or his hair, which had receded sharply on the sides, leaving a thick strip just in the middle of the brow, so that his hairline spelled *M* as he bent over his crossword. There was a Chinese expression for a couple like this: *A rose, decorating poop.* Surely the minister was aware of the physical disparity, but he was not grateful, bashful, or attentive. Instead, at dinner, he would say, "While you're up . . . " and raise his empty plate in the air. His wife was sitting when he did this. Was it a joke? Neither laughed. His wife got up and filled his plate and sat down again, quietly.

"A hundred bucks for walking a dog," repeated Mr. Bob. He gave a low whistle. Mr. Bob, of course, rendered all of his services for free. And his was a perennial position. As soon as he fixed the minister's toilet, the sink would lime up because the minister had forgotten to add the water-softener pellets for six months, or the mildew would return to the baseboards in the bathroom because the children had forgotten to put the fan on since the last time Mr. Bob had scrubbed it off, on his hands and knees. The minister's wife had recently been locked out of the house again, and Mr. Bob had arrived in ten minutes with his spare key. "You thaved the day," she told him, but before the day was over—before Mr. Bob had finished his supper, even—baby George had toddled out into the street again, and they were in the throes of another emergency. There was no improvement in their lives to show for all his aid, and Mr. Bob was not sure that any of them liked him: they found him useful. Yet he was drawn to them, to their quagmire, somehow, as he might be compelled to worry and work at a stubborn knot.

And he admired the minister, who read Greek and Hebrew, whose sermons were cold displays of a kind of knowledge that was foreign to Mr. Bob because it was abstract and impractical. Yes, he admired the minister without much liking him, which, he supposed, was the case with most of the congregation.

After Mr. Bob had received his instructions about the plants and the litter box and the mail and paper, the minister called the children in, and they and the minister and the minister's wife and Mr. Bob sat around the table, with its linoleum cloth cover still sticky with jelly and English muffin crumbs and dried splatters of the minister's special vodka tomato sauce. They held hands and began to pray. The minister prayed that it wouldn't rain on their vacation, and Ruthie prayed for cheesecake ice cream. Jacob prayed to get the backseat. Marcy prayed that Jacob and Paul wouldn't be mean to her again, and then one of them pinched her, but it couldn't be determined which, so the prayer was cut short and all three were punished and sent to bed without private reading.

When the children and the minister's wife had filed upstairs to the bedrooms, Mr. Bob was left alone with the minister.

"The world is certainly full of trouble these days," said Mr. Bob pointedly.

The minister tamped down his tobacco.

"I used to smoke a pipe now and then," said Mr. Bob.

"Want some? I don't have another pipe, though."

"No, forget it. It's bad for my nerves."

"That's what I thought."

"So, this morning," said Mr. Bob, "I read about a girl in Lebanon, eight years old. I guess a rocket hit the family car and both her parents and what not. And her face was all bandaged," he drew his hands back over his cheeks.

The minister sucked on his pipe. "Mmn," he said. He sat in his recliner and pushed the footrest out and made himself perfectly comfortable.

"My ankle's been swollen," said Mr. Bob. "I don't know why."

The minister leaned forward. "You want my chair?"

"No. It just reminded me."

Mr. Bob sat gingerly on the sofa. It was a white and light blue striped number but so dirty that you had to strain to see the pattern. He'd often stared at it, wondering how they had managed to get it quite this dirty. Had the children actually walked on it? Had a plant spilled, and then perhaps Baby George had rubbed the dirt into the fabric?

"You don't like rain, huh?" he asked the minister.

"What's that?"

"So, you really don't like rain when you're camping."

The minister laughed. "Listen, Mr. Bob. You and I believe in the same God, do we not?"

Mr. Bob shifted uncomfortably. He'd grown up in the church, but there were things about it that had always bothered him, among them a tacit agreement to profess belief in things that were objectively nonsense, and providence—an absurdly detailed providence in which God might decide whether or not it rained on one's camping trip—was one of these.

He supposed he didn't understand it. He believed in a God who was merely *looking on* at the human drama. Even if one agreed that He tried to involve Himself, His attentions would be—were, you could say, because you could see evidence of this—random and ineffectual. As Mr. Bob's were in the minister's life.

The minister was a smart man (perhaps brilliant, though Mr. Bob was no judge of this). Yet the minister would not admit that the silly prayers were only for the sake of the smaller children. He would not admit any *doubt* that God would hear and respond to a prayer about fudge.

"Well, here you have a war going on," Mr. Bob began, "and innocent civilians being killed all over the place, and we could go on to AIDS and civil war and starving in Africa and whatnot. . . . " Here he paused to try to remember what he'd been reading about the Sudan, but the article was from one of the minister's magazines, and if he got into it the minister might turn it around on him somehow, so instead he continued, "which I could be more precise about if you want me to. And then you have your family praying for a GameCube!"

The minister looked at him placidly. "God is infinite," he said.

"You give Him a fine bunch of things to consider," said Mr. Bob. "Nobody could concern themselves with all those petty things."

"*Nobody* could," smiled the minister. "But God could." And he put his pipe in its little stand, and went to the porch, and gathered the fat little beagle in his arms, sitting cross-legged on the floor with it, scratching its ears and reaching for his guitar, which he balanced on the floor in front of the dog as he began to strum.

MAKE ONE DOG HAPPY!

"You recognize that, Mr. Bob?"

"I don't," he admitted.

"It's 'Make Someone Happy.' You know that song, don't you?"

MAKE JUST ONE, ONE DOG HAPPY, ONE DOG THAT CHEERS YOU . . .

Mr. Bob had not recognized the song "Make Someone Happy" because there was no discernible melody when the minister sang. His wife, on the other hand, sang beautifully, but she would do so only in the privacy of the upstairs bedrooms as the children went off to sleep.

ONE DOG THAT LIGHTS WHEN IT'S NEAR YOU, ONE DOG YOU'RE EVERYTHING TOOOO . . .

The minister laid down his guitar to scratch the dog's belly. It rolled over and shut its little eyes, and one hind leg bobbed up and down.

Mr. Bob looked on in disgust at this display of mutual pleasuring. The minister's wife came downstairs and patted Mr. Bob's arm as she sat next to him, with two skeins of yarn and a page of directions.

"I dethided to try knitting," she said. "Now I'm not sure that I need one more thing to keep track of. Baby George got into it yethterday, and it took half an hour to roll up again."

LOVE IS THE ANSWER! SOME DOG TO LOVE IS THE ANSWER!

"You need a basket for those things," Mr. Bob said loudly. "Then always take a minute to put it on a high shelf. Just like with your keys." Mr. Bob had screwed in a hook for her, right inside the front door. "You always put them on the hook and now you know where they are."

ONCE YOU'VE FOUND HER, BUILD YOUR WORLD AROUND HERRRR . . .

"Oh piffle," she sighed, pulling at the yarn. "It's the tension I can't get the hang of."

"Shhh," said the minister, patting the fat little dog on its head. And they fell silent. The cicadas thrummed through the open windows. And the minister's froggy voice filled the room.

MAKE JUST ONE, ONE DOG HAPPY . . . AND YOU WILL BE HAPPY TOOOO.

The minister's wife sighed. "He loves that beagle," she whispered.

It seemed true. There was the minister, a man whose eyes darted back and forth as you spoke to him as if he were thinking of something else entirely, a man who ate his Christmas dinner in two minutes flat and left the table without excusing himself, a man whose only display of affection toward his children seemed to be patting them rather stiffly on the head. And his wife? Sometimes as she sat in a chair the minister would approach from the back and squeeze her shoulders roughly, which made her wince. "If you relax, it won't hurt as much," the minister would say.

But between the dog and the minister, there was tenderness.

———————

The day after the family's departure, Mr. Bob, arriving to bring in the morning paper, found a note on the minister's door: YOUR DOG WAS HOWLING 3:15 AM–5:00 AM!

After a small blank space, the note continued: AS YOU KNOW MY WIFE'S EXPECTING. ITS VERY IMPORTANT SHE GETS SLEEP AND THIS MAKES HER EMOTIONAL!!!! SHE'S

There was an arrow at the bottom of the page, "Over," and on the other side: PAST HER DUE DATE AND IF SHE GOES INTO LABOR MISSING AN ENTIRE NIGHTS SLEEP SHE COULD NEED EPIDURAL.

The writing became tiny in order to fit the rest on the page: WHICH HAVE RISKS INVOLVED WITH THEM. SHE HAS ALREADY COMPLETED FORMS REQUESTING NATURAL CHILDBIRTH.

Mr. Bob entered the house. The cat snaked around his legs madly as he stepped over some toy dump trucks and a plastic pony with a pink synthetic mane, through the house and back to the porch, where the dog lay on its side, panting in its crate. There was a terrible smell coming from the crate, and the newspaper lining was soaked with urine.

After rummaging around for a pair of dish gloves, Mr. Bob opened the door of the dog's cage in order to clean up after it. The dog gave a few little rolls to its side to gain momentum. Then, finally accomplishing the half revolution, it shot out of the crate on its squat little legs, ignoring Mr. Bob completely in favor of a piece of molding food that had dropped beneath the picnic table. Mr. Bob picked up the tag on its collar and inspected it. Rabies. No name or phone number.

He could not understand why, if they were so worried about losing the dog that he was not even entrusted to walk it, they would *not bother* to put their phone number and name on the tag. But this was their way. This was why Baby George had learned to unlock the front door and wandered out into the street. And they had gotten all upset and excited about it, yet upon his safe return had *simply not bothered* to change the lock until Mr. Bob, after being called to the search party a second time, had changed it for them.

When the dog was done scavenging, it clicked and jingled its way from one corner to the next, nose to the ground. It was hard to imagine this dog howling, so void it seemed of emotion. Mr. Bob's family had owned a German shepherd when he was young, a gentle beast that seemed to smile as it panted. It had wagged its tail madly when petted, even bowing its head in some odd mix of shame and reverence.

It occurred to Mr. Bob, watching the beagle rush madly around the porch and nose the corners, that this particular dog was very different, very like the minister, absorbed with his current book, or with the particular tense or case ending or what-have-you involved in some translation, or with his electronic chess game. In a way, he admired the focus.

After he'd fed the dog and lined the crate with fresh paper, Mr. Bob decided to check up on the dog walker. He had a few church members programmed in his cell phone, but not the private and his parents. It took him ten minutes to locate the laminated church phone tree that was usually affixed to the minister's refrigerator. He remembered, finally, that he had seen the list in a strange place while getting the dish gloves to clean the cage for the dog, and when he ducked his head into the cabinet, he noticed a steady leak from the drainpipe.

The minister had clearly seen the leak, and the laminated phone list had been his only remedy. He had not even thought to use a dishpan to catch the accumulation. The list now floated on a quarter inch of water in the bottom of the cabinet.

When Mr. Bob finished draining the cabinet with old towels, wringing the towels out and hanging them to dry on a rack, and rustling up a dishpan to catch the drips, it was eleven A.M. He then placed the call to the private, whose mother had to wake him up.

"Have you been walking the dog?" asked Mr. Bob.

"Huh?"

"The dog, the beagle you're sitting for—did you walk it yesterday?"

"Oh! Oh yeah! I'll go over there. Yeah . . . they gave me a key."

"Young man," said Mr. Bob firmly, "did you actually walk the dog yesterday?"

"Oh . . . sure. Yeah, I walked it," he said, still not bothering to sound any more awake than he was.

"May I speak to your mother, please?" said Mr. Bob.

When the mother got on the phone, Mr. Bob explained about the irate note. "The dog howls when it has to urinate," he explained, "and the woman next door is expecting a baby any day," he added, "which makes it especially important for her to sleep and so on."

"Yes . . . " She lowered her voice. "Dean just got back from Iraq, you know."

Mr. Bob paused. "Did he agree to walk the dog or not?"

His mother exhaled loudly. "I can't believe this," she mumbled.

"You see, the woman's husband left a note—"

"I'm not interested," she said coldly, as if he'd called to sell her something. "Good-bye."

Mr. Bob scooped the cat litter clean of lumps and taped a note to the front door: Dean, Please call one of the numbers below to let me know that you've walked the dog. You may also leave a message on my home answering machine or my cellular telephone answering machine.

Then Mr. Bob tried to forget about the dog. He did his grocery shopping, driving by the house again on his way home. His note was still taped to the front door. He passed by the nursing home to check on his mother, who was sleeping in front of her television with the baseball game on, her White Sox cap pulled over her eyes and her fuzzy white hair sticking out the sides like a clown's wig.

As his mother nodded in her waterproof recliner, Mr. Bob pulled up a folding chair and turned off the sound and sat next to her, as if they were enjoying some wholesome family time together. It was a game that took his mind off things for a bit, if only because it was thoroughly maddening to him. The team had been fine all season, playing well until the All-Star break, when, predictably, they went into a tailspin. And now, when it was important to reverse the momentum, all the scrubs were in as they played Kansas City, who was thirty games back of first place. The Sox scored, and then the pitcher let go and Kansas City scored two, and it was back and forth every inning, until Mr. Bob got up and shut off the television in disgust.

He sat in silence, debating whether he should wake his mother. She had been a fine, lively person all of her life but had turned very grouchy and forgetful. He visited every day, yet he'd heard her tell the other residents that she had a son who never came to see her.

Suddenly he found himself up again, turning the set back on, just to check the progress. The problem, he thought, with baseball, was that there was too much of it. You had to be a busy person. Things had to take your attention away. Or perhaps, as his mother did, you might enjoy it if you could sleep through most of it, waking only to see a batter here and there, a particular play here and there, and drowse back into oblivion—a place in which there was no score, and no result, and no play-offs to make or fail to make, and no end of the season. Otherwise, there was too much to be suffered through.

The game, such an easy one to win, theoretically, stretched into extra innings, and then was lost in the last inning by the same closer who'd performed so brilliantly the previous year in the play-offs. The close-ups showed him swearing, with some expression that looked like "Fucky." It was a white pitcher, not one of the Venezuelans, so there was no chance it was something else he was saying, in Spanish or anything, and as Mr. Bob was puzzling over this, his mother woke up and announced that the nurses had been stealing the clothes in her closet again.

As he drove away from the nursing home, the loss of the game had its usual effect on Mr. Bob: it made him irritated with life in general. He could forget it for a moment, and then just as he had finally coaxed himself to think of something else, he began to have the sensation that something was rotten in the State of Denmark. Oh, yes! That humiliating loss! The stinking bull pen! And the stinking dog!

He suddenly felt the weight of the day's humiliation. He had been deemed incapable of a simple task and now was forced to sit around and worry as the young man took his sweet time in walking the dog. Nobody else was worried; it all fell to Mr. Bob.

As soon as Mr. Bob arrived in the minister's driveway and shut off his car, he could hear a low, plaintive howl coming from the back porch. At the neighbor's house, the porch light and the living room light were on.

Mr. Bob shut off his car and walked up to the porch. The note he'd left for the private remained. He would go inside, he thought, and try to quiet the dog. He would call the boy again. But when Mr. Bob opened the front door of the house, the howling stopped. On the porch, the dog stood quietly inside the dry cage, his tail thumping against the sides.

Mr. Bob stood in front of the dog's crate, his stomach churning. He didn't want to be at the mercy of the boy and the boy's mother and the dog and the minister. The fact was, he was a responsible man. And not infirm: he got up on the roof and cleaned his own gutters. He had even cleaned the minister's gutters, with no objections from the minister or the minister's wife. And now he was not fit enough to walk a dog!

This thought made him angry enough to do what he realized he had come to do in the first place. He opened the cage, clipped on the leash, and out the door they went, the dog straining madly, pulling Mr. Bob forward down the sidewalk toward the park.

It was true that the dog was strong.

The park sat on ten acres of land left to the university, which had reconstructed an Illinois "prairie"—long, waxy, amber and reddish grasses circumscribed by a paved walking path. There was even a lagoon on the far side, but the overall natural effect was spoiled because there were huge new houses on the edge of the lagoon, brick on the front but aluminum on the side (as if, Mr. Bob thought, all visitors would approach head-on and would lack peripheral vision). Scattered here and there on the sides of the walking path were strange sculptures: nude statues, stacks of tires with glitter on them, and a skewered Dodge Dart hovering ten feet off the ground—all student art projects from the university.

After relieving itself, the dog began to trot as fast as Mr. Bob would allow it. Whenever she caught a scent, she strained to go after it, and Mr. Bob pulled her back. As they went on, they developed a rhythm, the dog veering off the paved path and Mr. Bob pulling it on, the steady click click of the dog's nails on the path, veering again, pulling, click click.

And Mr. Bob began to relax. The dog was strong but not stronger than he was, and the night—now in its final orange and pink dusk—was warm but finally, for the first time in a week, not unpleasant, with the humidity rising up from the prairie in a cloud of mist and the grasshoppers popping up from the grass whenever the dog strayed into it. He felt the slight thrill of doing something unusual and slightly forbidden. A nightly walk like this might do him some good, he thought. After the minister returned, he might offer to walk the dog each evening.

So it was the rhythm, the pleasant night, the future hopes, maybe, that caused him to relax his hold on the leash. Or perhaps it would have happened anyway. But in any case, as Mr. Bob and the dog rounded a bend, they were suddenly in full view of a bench with something dark and violent-looking on it. Mr. Bob froze. No, it was not violence, it was . . . ah, the students had come back this week! And already they were at it, these two on the bench, fondling madly. And as Mr. Bob tried to decide how to pass through this gauntlet (the path was not wide enough that he could avoid it, and he'd come too far to turn around), the leash must have slackened just a little more. And in that very moment—because, perhaps, the dog had been sensing this slackening, or, more likely, because it caught, just at that moment, a particular musk for which it lusted more than anything in the world—the dog gave a sudden sharp yank on the leash.

And that was that. The leash just slipped off of Mr. Bob's hand,

and the dog was off, into the long grasses of the prairie. For a few moments, he could see it, the tail arcing like a dolphin's fin in the ocean of prairie grass, up and down, until suddenly the movement ceased.

"Oh, noooo!" wailed Mr. Bob, and the grass shivered in response.

"Help! My dog!" he yelled, turning back toward the lovers' bench, but it was empty.

There was no choice but to turn and run, to wade as best he could, through the field. When he reached the middle, the prairie grass came up to his rib cage, and the ground was full of tiny lumps and holes, the kind that could twist or break an ankle, and he shuffled through it madly, trying as hard as he could to discern the path that the dog had made.

But it was no use; there was no trace of the dog, and the dusk had turned to evening, and Mr. Bob found himself in the middle of the prairie, straining for breath.

It was a beautiful night. There was a sharp, bright slice of moon, and fireflies winked on and off among the Queen Anne's lace—a beautiful night, in the middle of such trouble! Proof, thought Mr. Bob, that God carries on his merry business, leaving us alone in the midst of our troubles.

It was late. It was now illegal to be in the park, and Mr. Bob felt exposed and slightly frightened. He would go back to the minister's house and call someone to help look for the dog. But who? There was the laminated church phone list, of course. And some of those numbers were programmed in his cellular telephone, right here in his pocket.

But any church member he might ask to help would also relate the story to the minister. He could not ask them *not* to relate it, and this meant he would have to explain that he'd walked the dog and lost it, after the minister—rightly so, as it turned out—had not entrusted him with the dog in the first place.

Mr. Bob returned to the minister's house. He looked up numbers for the Humane Society and the local dog pounds (there were two) and underlined them. Then he closed the phone book and sat in the minister's favorite chair.

There was a buzz. Had he turned on the massage feature on the recliner? He fiddled with some buttons near the cup holder until he realized that the sound was his own telephone, vibrating in his pocket.

"Hello?"

"Hi, Mithter Bob, you weren't thleeping?" It was the minister's wife. "We're just checking in. Everyone's thwimming right now, and I'm trying to get Baby George down first, before they all pile in."

"You're in a hotel? Did you give up on camping then?"

"Well, it's been raining. Everything we own got thoaked yesterday because we pitched the tent at an angle, so there was a puddle that got into one of the thleeping bags, and oh, my gosh, Mr. Bob, I can't tell you. It's been horrible."

"Oh," said Mr. Bob. "That's too bad."

"Is everything okay there?"

"Well . . . " said Mr. Bob. His palms had begun to sweat. "Actually—"

"Oh, no," her voice turned shrill. "What happened? Is everything okay?"

"Well you know, I wasn't in charge, actually, but it's about the dog."

"Just a minute, Mr. Bob, I'm going in the bathroom so Baby George doesn't . . . Okay, here we are, so it's only the dog, you said?"

She said this so lightly and easily that he was taken aback.

"Actually," he said, "The young man didn't come last night, and then it wet its crate."

"Well, that doesn't thurprise me. It's incontinent."

"Oh, is that so?"

"Yes. It's a *terrible* dog."

"Really?"

"Well, don't you think so?"

"I suppose I see what you mean, yes."

She lowered her voice. "I can't *thhh-tand* it."

"You can't?"

She sighed. "I know it's wrong. But who do you think has to clean up all the puddles?"

"You do? Well, I suppose that's not right."

"No, it isn't right! I have five kids, Mr. Bob! Five dressers to change over every theason and five schedules to keep up and all that laundry and two kids in diapers, and I just *could not believe it* when my own husband brought home an incontinent beagle! As if I needed something else to take care of!"

He was trying to think why she said two kids were in diapers. Wasn't Ruthie five already? Had they simply forgotten to train her?

There was a hiccup.

"Are you crying?"

Silence.

"Oh . . . " said Mr. Bob. "Maybe it's the altitude affecting you."

She sniffed. "In Iowa? Is it high altitude here?"

"Well," he said, "camping in general. It's stressful."

"I'll thay. Except for him! He does his *thtudying*, but I . . . "

And she began to sob.

It broke his heart. He wanted only to help her, to fix whatever was wrong, and he realized this impulse was probably behind everything else he did for them: the chores, the cleaning, the house-sitting.

"Don't cry!" he said. "About the dog. There's something . . . "

The sobbing stopped. "What?"

Here was an opportunity to tell the truth, appearing before him like an open lane of traffic, if he could simply move without hesitation. Then another car wove into the open space and the opportunity was gone. He said, "I can take care of it for you."

"Oh. Well," she said, "it *is* very old. It could die and no one would question it."

"Yes," he said. Did she think he'd offered to kill the dog? Yes, she thought so and was not appalled.

But what was the difference, really? The dog was gone; it would not come back. They had both said this about beagles. They had no sense of loyalty. And in this version, he would never have to confess to anyone that he'd lost it accidentally. And here he suddenly felt lucky in a way that he'd thought was reserved for people like the minister. Something had fallen into his lap.

"You might tell your family that you talked to me today," he said gently, "and that I came to check the mail, and because of how hot it's been . . . "

"And because the dog was very old," she continued.

"I just found it, lying there."

She drew a sharp breath. "But I'm afraid," she whispered. "I don't want you to, I don't want—"

"You'll never know any details," he told her, feeling brave now, chivalrous. "You'll just come home, and it will be . . . gone. How would that be?"

"Oh, God forgive me!"

"He does. I'm sure He does."

There was a little hum over the wire. It was just possible to make out someone else's voice. It seemed like an argument, a low voice, yelling, followed by a whine. He did not know if she could hear it, too.

Finally she said, in a false, light tone, "Are the plants fine? And the cat's okay?"

"The cat leaves a very full litter box, but I suppose that's normal. And the plants are good. And there was a little leak in the drainpipe, under the sink, I don't know if you noticed. I cleaned it all up and the plumber is coming tomorrow."

"Oh, Mr. Bob," she said, ardently, "what would we do without you?"

That was a question he'd been waiting to hear. It made it all worth his trouble.

Shortly after Mr. Bob had put his cell phone back on Keyguard and inserted it in his pocket, and just after he'd decided to go home and try to sort through what he seemed to have promised the minister's wife, the minister's doorbell rang. Mr. Bob was not sure if he wanted to answer it. What would he do if it were someone in the neighborhood, with the dog in hand?

It was the private. "Hey, man," he said.

"Hello. Are you—"

"Here for the dog," he said.

The private might be a fine person to search the neighborhood for the lost dog. But how could Mr. Bob ask him? He had come too late.

"I have bad news," said Mr. Bob. "The dog passed away."

"Oh, it—for real?"

Mr. Bob nodded gravely. As if to betray his mendacity, his nose began to run, and he shoveled in his pocket for a handkerchief. There was only the cell phone and a receipt from the Meijer grocery store.

"You're kidding. You're kidding," said the private, shaking his head dumbly. "You mean it's dead, actually?"

"Hmmn, afraid so. Yes."

"For real?"

"Well, he was very old. Eleven! Old for a dog. Of that breed." Then he wondered if eleven was merely old for a German shepherd. He knew nothing of beagles. Maybe the minister's wife didn't either. They might live to be twenty.

"Aw, fuck me," said the private. Mr. Bob tried to hold in his shock at this expression, though he now realized that it was the same expression that the Sox reliever had used earlier, in the baseball game he'd watched at the nursing home. When the private said it, it was gentle almost, plaintive, and sounded more like "Ah, me" than "Fuck me."

"It just *died*?"

"It's not—"

And here, because the private had misted up a little, Mr. Bob had to stop himself lest he begin to cry too, because it had been a long night, and he had only ever wanted to help; he had not meant to have these troubles.

"I can dig the grave for you."

"A grave? Oh, of course, I thought of that," said Mr. Bob, who'd thought of no such thing. When his mother had put the German shepherd down, they'd left her at the vet's office.

"I can dig a grave," insisted the private. "It's no problem."

"No need," said Mr. Bob cheerfully.

Then the private just stood there, waiting in the open door. But for what?

He was very short, noticed Mr. Bob. His hair stuck straight up and gleamed with some kind of pomade, and he wore a shirt with the arms cut off that read Little Learner's Nursery School. His mother's shirt? His sister's? In any case, the sleeves had been cut off to reveal his arms, which were very thick. It was as if the muscles there were meant to make up in manliness what he lacked in height. And his little chest was lifted, suspended there. He wanted Mr. Bob to say something.

"I was in Korea in the early sixties," said Mr. Bob, "but that was peacekeeping."

"Oh."

"I was assigned to an acting troupe. That was actually . . . I had fun with it."

"Oh."

Mr. Bob did not know what to say. He never did. He was inadequate to all human relations; he had never understood them and so had never married, he thought, and so had friends in the church, all of whom he suspected were simply putting up with him because it was the Christian thing to do.

"Well, I appreciate it, certainly, your offer of help with the dog," said Mr. Bob. "But no."

"It's okay," said the private, and he lunged forward and hugged Mr. Bob tightly. No one had hugged Mr. Bob tightly for a very long time. The private smelled of smoke, and liquor, and fabric softener: a romantic, young-person, lonely-night smell. It filled Mr. Bob with a terrible mix of discomfort and longing.

"Well!" Mr. Bob said brightly, pulling away, his hand grabbing the doorknob, "Thanks . . . for your service to our country!"

"It's okay, man," said the private glumly. "Take it easy."

Working by flashlight, Mr. Bob scratched a shallow grave in the minister's backyard. He found two pieces of kindling in the garage, nailed together a cross, and stuck it in the ground he'd disturbed. And then he went home, took off his wet clothes, showered, and went to bed.

As Mr. Bob lay between his clean sheets, in clean pajamas, he wondered what to do if the dog did return, or if the pound had found it. He supposed he would have to take care of it in the way that the minister's wife suggested. It would be easy. He would call the vet in the next town, where the minister wouldn't go, and say he needed to have his dog put down because it was eleven and incontinent. He would carry the dog in his arms, as if it were infirm, and, with a long face, hand it to some receptionist. No one would be the wiser.

But the image of himself carrying the fat little dog in his arms recalled his mother (who was small now but had once been formidable, broad shouldered, lifting bales of hay and calves and ewes in her arms) carrying the German shepherd to the lawn to relieve itself, and later, hoisting it up into that light blue pickup truck they'd had and into the vet's office. She'd turned, shaking her head violently as she walked out, so quickly that he'd had to run to keep up with her.

Was the beagle such a terrible dog? Perhaps, had Mr. Bob taken a moment to pat the dog on the head, or speak kindly to it, it would not have left. In any case, if the dog was incontinent, it had only howled in the evening because it was alone, not because it had to relieve itself. This seemed so pitiful that Mr. Bob felt some atavistic desire to howl himself. But he turned out his light and tossed and turned for hours before sleep would come.

In the daylight, Mr. Bob checked with the two vets' offices, the Humane Society, and the dog pound, leaving his home number with them. And then he began to search. He caught a glimpse of something squat and short creeping along an alley on Green Street near the university. But it was Welcome Week and the returning girls from Presby House were sponsoring a Fair Trade sidewalk sale, and by the time he got around all their hoohah, the thing had disappeared.

In the parking lot of the Café Paradiso, he thought he heard the click of a dog's nails on the cobbled bricks, but when he followed the sound back to the dumpster, it was suddenly quiet, except for some Bob Dylan music drifting out of the café. He stood and listened for a moment, wondering why, after they'd all stopped liking this kind of music, they had taken it up again.

"Have you seen a stray beagle?" he asked in the little stores and magazine stands, at the taco cart by the student union. And the kids were concerned and solicitous, and he felt some sickening sense of guilt that he was not just looking for the dog but hunting it. And when, finally, he gave up looking, he still felt in every quiet place that the dog was lurking there, accusing him.

On the day the family was scheduled to return, Mr. Bob went to the minister's house. He took in the paper and the mail, watered the plants, and scooped the cat litter. As he did this he had the giddy feeling of getting away with something: he had made the minister's wife happy, and it had been accomplished with no premeditation on his part.

Part of his giddiness came from nerves, of course, because he was not out of it yet, and he tried to anticipate the minister's questions: "How much water did you give her? Did she seem ill? What time did you find her?"

Mr. Bob picked some of the tiger lilies that flanked the air conditioner, wrapped the ends in wet paper towels, and placed them on the dog's grave. Then he went to inspect the front of the house. In the lawn next door, a big sign read IT'S A GIRL, WELCOME HOME ABBEY ROSE. One of the pink balloons festooning the sign had come loose and blew toward his feet. As he bent to pick it up, the minister's red van turned down the street.

It was not the right picture, Mr. Bob thought—the happy sign and the balloons. But as he stood there on the lawn, nervously hiding the pink balloon behind him, the doors of the van opened, and the children piled out and embraced him. The minister opened his door, approached Mr. Bob gravely, and hugged him too.

"Mr. Bob," said the minister. "It's okay. We forgive you."

"This flew off the sign next door," said Mr. Bob, waving the balloon, but the children ignored him and clung to his legs and pulled on his arms:

"We forgive you, Mr. Bob," parroted Marcy, and Paul, and Ruthie, and even Baby George: "I fow giffu," although when he was done, he stuck out his tongue. And it took Mr. Bob a moment to wonder what they forgave him for, exactly, since the story they knew was that he had merely found the dog lying there.

Jacob yelled from inside the van. "You locked me in!"

"Jacob," said the minister, "just pull harder." But he went back anyway to help him, and Mr. Bob was surprised to notice as the minister pulled at the door that his back was not quite as erect as he'd pictured it. There was that small slump between the shoulders that is common to very tall people.

The minister's wife caught Mr. Bob's eye and gave a quick flash of a smile.

She was happy, very happy! Mr. Bob winked at her. She blushed and made herself busy with the luggage. But the minister took her arm. "The bags can wait," he said. "Let's see where the dog is buried."

They filed into the backyard and joined hands, as they did nightly at the dinner table over the sticky linoleum tablecloth.

"Dear Lord," said the minister, "we know you make every decision. We know you have a greater plan and a greater wisdom. For in—"

And Marcy screamed. And the children dropped their hands and crouched down to the ground and were screaming.

For there was the dog, risen from the dead. It scrambled into the backyard, wagging its tail, nosing its way around them, the blue leash still hanging from its collar. Mr. Bob was horrified, "I only . . . I . . ."

But the minister was not waiting for Mr. Bob to say anything. He only hugged the dog, with his eyes closed, and whispered some private prayer under his breath.

His wife tucked her chin, her mouth puckering as if she'd swallowed something bitter. Mr. Bob knew that it was more than this one defeat that stung her. The minister had been blessed, and she had not, and Mr. Bob, having failed her, had not; and some things could not be changed. Call it what you would—providence, or God's will, or the extraordinary golden luck that seems to fall on some people—the minister, having always gotten what he wanted, would continue to get what he wanted. And the minister expected this, so much so that it didn't seem strange to him that a dog that should never have been able to come back, came back. It happened for him, as everything did. And this, the minister believed, was the hand of a God who cared about his every comfort and happiness. Surely, the minister even believed that it was God's will working through his wife, and through Mr. Bob, and through every single person who catered to him and made his life softer.

It was not fair. Yet, thought Mr. Bob, his belief is genuine. Maybe this is a start. Maybe you begin, he thought, as he watched the minister on his knees by the grave, by following someone who knows how to be credulous. And he put out his hand and helped the minister to his feet.

Alewives

Allison was the death of things. She took the class hamster home for spring vacation, and her dog knocked over its aquarium and killed it. A month later, she let this same dog outside without closing the fence in the yard; it ran out onto the highway and got hit by a car.

"Allison, Allison," her father would sigh, shaking his head. Her grandfather, before he had moved to Florida, had said her name in the same way, only after he said it, he would take her on his lap. "Do you know why I tease you?" he'd ask. "Because I like you. That's why."

But Allison's father never told her that.

Allison left her guitar on the floor of the foyer, and her mother tripped over it and broke her leg. She got a cast with a flat disc on the bottom that reminded Allison of the Chinese bound feet she had seen in a PBS special. In the special, the Chinese women walked on these discs in short steps, like dainty wind-up dolls, but Allison's mother lumbered heavily, heaving her cast leg forward, then dragging her good one after it, her large arms swinging in violent accompaniment. She was lumbering like this into the kitchen now, to get ready for company.

"Should we make dessert?" she yelled to Allison's father, who was sitting in the living room with Allison.

Allison's father folded back a page of his magazine.

"Should we make dessert?" she yelled again.

"Do what you want," he mumbled.

"Well, are they dessert eaters?"

Her father didn't answer.

"Do they eat dessert?" she asked.

Allison went into the kitchen and ducked under her mother's legs, which were planted in front of the open refrigerator. She grabbed a bunch of celery from the crisper, took it to the sink, and began washing it with orange antibiotic dish liquid and a vegetable brush.

"We wouldn't know!" her mother proclaimed to the open refrigerator. "They never have us over!" She pushed the door shut and lumbered to middle of the room. There she made a small grunt and bent over, leaning her elbows on the kitchen island and breathing heavily.

"She doesn't cook!" yelled Allison's dad.

"Who doesn't cook?"

"*She* doesn't!"

"Yes, but who *doesn't cook*?"

"Some people don't cook!"

Allison had taken a knife and was filling the celery—generously—with peanut butter.

"Good God," said her mother, "is that all for you?"

Allison put the celery on a plate and went to the living room, where she sat by her father and began to eat.

"Allison," he said, "do you have to chew so loud?"

It tasted terrible anyway, so she dumped the rest in the wastebasket.

Then she sat back on the sofa and watched the News Hour while her father removed *Wine for Dummies* from the bookshelf, put it in a drawer, and rearranged the books that remained, standing back a few times to look at them. When he finished, he shifted Allison's current school picture behind an older one, in which she was very little and playing dress-up in a pair of high-heeled shoes. Then he disappeared upstairs. The poet laureate came on the News Hour and started to recite something.

"Are you watching that?" her mother yelled.

"Yes," answered Allison.

"Where's your father?"

"Upstairs," Allison said.

"Then shut it off," said her mother. "It's giving me a headache."

Allison went upstairs to her little brother's room and peeked inside. He'd been put to bed an hour ago and was breathing deeply. One of his arms hung out of the crib slats, and his Teletubby nested in the crook of the other. Allison left, got the camera from the den, then snuck back in and took a picture of him. When the flash went off, he sat up and started crying.

Allison pulled the door shut quickly and replaced the camera. Then she joined her mother downstairs at the breakfast nook where she was seated, peeling onions.

"Why's the baby up?" said her father, as he came downstairs. He was wearing a new shirt and his hair was still wet. Allison could smell his soap from the kitchen. Allison's mother could not shower. She could only sponge off with a bag around her leg, and then it was what she called "a process." Tonight she was wearing her glasses and a blue tee-shirt dress and sandals without nylons. She had worn a tee-shirt dress almost every day since Baby Ben had been born.

"Is the baby *up*?" she said. When she peeled onions, her face turned red and broke out in beads of sweat. "Why on earth?"

She picked up an onion brusquely, as if she might throw it. "Well, I'm not doing him any favors by getting him," she said. "He'll have to put himself back to sleep."

"I'll help with the onions," said Allison to her mother.

"No thanks, sweetheart," her mother sighed. "It'll go faster this way."

Allison's dad turned the television back on then, and Allison went to join him.

By the time company arrived at seven thirty, Allison's dad was in a better mood. Allison stood behind him as he opened the door for them. The man, Chuck, was her dad's cousin. He was bald and looked older than her dad. Allison's dad said that Chuck was a dope because he never finished his sentences. Allison's mom said that Allison's dad was just jealous because Chuck had gotten a divorce from his first wife and found a younger one. The younger one's name was Valerie. She was skinny, with short hair and a short skirt. She was too pretty to be married to a dope, especially an old and bald dope, but she didn't act embarrassed about it.

"You remember Allison," her dad said to Valerie.

"Oh!" said Valerie, "Allison! I didn't even recognize you!"

At Valerie and Chuck's wedding two years ago, Allison had been seven and a half. The band had played a song with her name in it, and at the time Allison thought maybe they had written it just for her. Chuck had asked Allison to dance with him. They hadn't really danced, though; Chuck had picked her up, then pumped her hand up and down in a pretend-dancing, and everyone at the wedding had gathered around, watching them. Allison was too heavy to be picked up now.

"Kids!" said Chuck, shaking his head. "They really . . . "

Valerie and Chuck went into the living room, and her dad shut off the television and poured Chuck a drink. Valerie couldn't have any liquor because her dad had been an alcoholic, and she didn't want iced tea because it was too late in the day for caffeine. Allison's mom offered ginger ale and 7UP, but the sugar in those things bothered Valerie, since she suspected that she was a borderline diabetic. Finally she decided on ice water.

"I hope shepherd's pie will be okay for dinner," said her mother. "Vegetarian special."

"Oh," said Valerie, knitting her brows, "the crust, too?"

Allison's mom turned as red as when she'd been peeling onions; it turned out that she had bought the crust for the shepherd's pie at a store. After she dug through the garbage for the label, she discovered that there was some animal fat in it, after all.

"It's okay, really," said Valerie, kindly. "I can splurge once in a while. I'm not extremely strict about things."

Allison's mom didn't say much at dinner, at first; it was her dad doing all the talking. "Are you enjoying yourselves?" he asked them.

Valerie took a sip of her water.

"What I mean," he said, "is, are you enjoying yourselves, living in there? Because once you have kids it's hassle-city, believe me."

"I couldn't move out of the city," said Valerie.

"If we start a family," said Chuck, touching Valerie's arm.

"I couldn't live out of the city," she repeated.

Allison's dad began to talk about square feet you could get out here as opposed to Lincoln Park or even somewhere snobby, like Evanston. You had the lakefront in Chicago, he said, but how often did you use it? They had a pool now, besides, and there never were any alewives in that. Allison's mother said that if anyone wanted seconds on anything, Allison's father would be glad to get up and serve them.

"Yes, ma'am," Allison's father said. Then he turned to Chuck and Valerie, flicked his wrist, and made a whoosh, like the sound of a whip, through his teeth. Chuck accepted a second portion, and Valerie shook her head, then put her napkin to her mouth and spit something into it quietly.

Allison's father came back from the kitchen with the shepherd's pie and cut Chuck a piece.

When Allison's father made a joke and nobody laughed, he always tried again, as if they hadn't heard it. Bowing to Allison's mom, he flicked his wrist and made the whipping sound again.

Allison's mother gave a tiny snort. Chuck took his plate from Allison's dad and said thank you very quietly. Valerie didn't laugh at all but looked down into her empty water glass.

Nobody said anything for what seemed like a long time.

"I want more, please," said Allison.

At that, everybody laughed very loudly. "Just a sliver," said Allison's mother.

Allison's father took her plate and cut a big piece, smiling and shrugging as he did so. "She likes her food," he said.

"Allison," said Valerie, "we hear you're very smart in school."

"She is," said Allison's mother. "They want to move her up a grade."

"Would you like that, Allison?" asked Valerie. "Or do you have friends in your class?"

Allison wondered if she should tell about the hamster. "Not at the moment," she said.

"Allison, Allison," sighed her dad.

Allison began eating her sliver of shepherd's pie. The crust tasted warm and buttery, and it made her feel better to eat it. Then she looked up, and everybody was watching her, so she put her fork down and folded her hands back on her lap.

"We have the best of both worlds here," said her father. "I just hop in the car and I'm downtown in twenty minutes."

"It took us an hour," said Valerie.

"Well, with traffic," said Allison's father.

"Traffic," Chuck agreed. "I'm sure that accounts for it."

"I pop over to the Art Institute or the Opera, for example, all the time," her father said.

"Oh?" said Valerie.

"Oh?" said Allison's mother.

"The, you know, the Lyric whatchacallit," said her father. "I had a subscription to that."

Then Allison's mother began to laugh so hard that no sound came out at all: she shook while her face contracted and her hand fanned her mouth. Chuck and Valerie smiled politely, while Allison's father shifted in his chair.

"He bought a season ticket, and he went to see one of them. One!" Now the simmer released itself: "Ha, haaaaa! Ha, haaaaa!" said her mother, bending forward to press at the corner of her eyes with her napkin.

Allison's father didn't look at her mother, and he didn't look at Valerie or Chuck. He didn't say anything.

"The next year, he bought bee hives! He put them in the backyard and bought a hat with a little net on it, for collecting honey! Oh, Lord! I wish I had a picture for you."

"You have the space for that kind of . . . " Chuck said, making loops in the air with one hand.

"He wants to run a marathon now," her mother continued. "Can you imagine?"

"We barely have room for Valerie's books in our place," said Chuck. "And if I want to watch television and she's reading . . . "

Allison's father had leaned his head back, as if he were inspecting a spot on the ceiling. The muscles stood out on the corner of his jaw. "You'll find out," he said. "When you have kids, you'll find out."

"I don't want kids," Valerie said.

"I'd like kids," said Chuck.

Allison tried to take another bite of crust. Her fork scraped her plate, and it was the only sound in the house. She picked out a wood knot in the table and studied it. She then imagined herself burping very loudly into the silence. That was funny. That helped for a second.

Then Allison's mother announced dessert time. Valerie told her to rest her leg and started for the kitchen.

Allison followed her. "I can help," she said.

Valerie put a hand on Allison's shoulder. She smelled like smoke and spearmint. "Of course you can," she said. "Show me where it is."

Allison showed Valerie the strawberries and ice cream that her mother had decided on for dessert. She gave Valerie a big spoon and watched as she ladled the berries into five bowls. Valerie wore impractical bracelets on her wrists that clinked together as she worked.

"What's a cradle robber?" Allison asked her.

Valerie put down the strawberry spoon and looked at Allison.

"What did she just say?" her mother yelled from the dining room.

"Allison! Allison!" yelled her father. "Get in here!"

Allison's face felt hot. She ran upstairs and into her bedroom with her heart pounding. *Cradle robber,* she thought, with a small flow of pleasure. She came out to hang over the railing and listen.

"It's okay," said Valerie. "She's a kid. She's just curious about it."

"I don't know where she heard it," Allison's mother said. "She must pick these things up at school."

"Of course," said Valerie.

"If she moves up a grade, it'll be worse."

"Hey," said Chuck, with a laugh, "I'm the old one, remember. If it doesn't bother me . . ."

"Well," said Allison's mother, taking a spoonful of ice cream, "We're all the old ones, technically. Excepting Valerie."

Valerie excused herself and went upstairs to the bathroom.

Allison ducked back into her bedroom, shut the door, and took her pants off. There was a red mark where her waistband had been pinching her. She couldn't hear Valerie peeing or flushing, but she could hear clinking downstairs; someone was doing the dishes and Chuck was laughing. Then they all were laughing. She lay on top of her covers in her underwear and her tee shirt and looked at the ceiling fan.

Closing her eyes, Allison pictured herself sneaking out the back door, picking tomatoes, then dropping them one by one over the upstairs railing into the kitchen. "What's that sound?" she imagined her mother saying as the tomatoes dropped steadily to the linoleum: splat, splat. As she thought of this, Allison lay shaking, laughing softly. Then the laugh ended, and while she lay empty and defenseless, a picture of Flip, the dog, came back into her head, hobbling back from the highway to lie on their stoop, his blood puddling out in a dark stain on the cement and her mother shrieking, "Allison! The dog! Good God! Allison!" And she could not think of anything she could do that might be funny enough to make it go away.

Through her open window she could hear Valerie and Chuck telling her parents thank you so much; next time they could meet at a restaurant in the city. Did they like Indian? That was Allison's father's favorite. Her mother wasn't sure if she'd had it before. Valerie's heels clicked on the driveway, and a car started up.

Downstairs, her mother wondered why Chuck was bothering putting Valerie through school. Didn't they know the job market was horrible for a Ph.D. these days? Her father said if you published enough you could always find work. Her mother wanted to know what he knew about it; he'd quit after only a quarter. Her father wanted to know whose fault that was. Her mother said it wasn't anybody's fault; it had saved him eight years of training for a job that didn't exist. Her father was getting ready to say something very unpleasant then, and he bet her mother would rather not hear it; and her mother said say it, and her father said that she wouldn't want to hear it, ever. It was that bad.

Her mother lumbered upstairs and into the bathroom. Allison followed her there.

"Allison," said her mother, as she lowered herself onto the pot, "could a body get some privacy around here?"

The front door slammed.

"Where's dad going?"

"Jogging," said her mother. She finished wiping and stayed on the toilet, head in hands, elbows on knees.

"It's late to be jogging," said Allison.

"He's in *train*ing," said her mother, not looking up.

"Oh," said Allison. She took a *Reader's Digest* from the magazine rack beside the toilet and opened it as she sat on the side of the tub. "Bose Acoustic Wave," she said, holding up the magazine, "We should get one of these. They're supposed to be good."

"I wouldn't mind jogging at night," said Allison's mom. "I never get asked, that's all."

"You have a broken foot," said Allison.

Allison's mother sighed. "That's right," she said. She motioned to Allison, and Allison came forward and took her mother under the armpits and helped her to stand up.

She smelled like sweat and Secret.

"I'm sorry I said cradle robber," said Allison.

Her mother planted a kiss on Allison's forehead. "You should treat others the way you want to be treated, Allison," she said. "Chuck and Valerie would never call you fat."

Allison sat back on the edge of the tub as her mother lumbered from the bathroom. Her face and throat were warm again, as if she'd been caught doing something bad, but without the pleased feeling that naughty things usually brought her. She wanted her grandfather. She wanted her grandfather to take her on his lap and say, "Bless your baby heart," but he was too far away to do that anymore. The tightness lowered to her torso; it felt like someone had put a rubber band around her ribcage. She stood up and looked at her face in the bathroom mirror, but she only saw Allison the way Allison always looked, and she couldn't tell if her mother and people at school were right about it after all, and then her eyes were filling with liquid and blurring it all up.

She wiped her face and pulled her tee shirt down over her underwear. Then she went downstairs and pulled a chair up to the mantle and reached behind her baby picture to her school photo. She stood on the chair and looked at it. What had happened was that her eyes had gotten very small compared to her face. Even as she watched, the flesh in the picture face seemed to expand stealthily toward the edges of the frame, like pancake batter on a griddle.

Allison replaced the school photo behind the baby one, then took down her parents' wedding picture. Allison's mother had long blonde hair in the photo and the same pink skin. She wore a wide-brimmed white hat, and she was grinning and clutching at her father's arm with both hands. Her father looked exactly the same; he was handsome. He was more handsome than her mother was, even then. He smiled in the picture like he always smiled, with no change in his eyes, like he was showing his teeth to the dentist.

Stepping down from the chair, Allison eased the wedding photo from its cardboard backing. Then she took a pencil from the coffee table and drew a small black dot on one of her father's teeth, replaced the photo in the cardboard, and put it up onto the mantle, between two pictures of their trips to Lake Michigan. In one, her mom was pregnant with Baby Ben. Allison was very little, and her father held her hand at the edge of the water. In the other, no one was swimming or even wading, because there was a stripe of dead, silvery white fish littering the shoreline as far as you could see.

You could take alewives in a bucket, she thought, and dump them into the swimming pool: "The pool, Allison, goddamnit, the pool!" It might be funny.

It might be, but she wished instead that somehow you could go to a place where if you ruined things or broke somebody's leg it was because you wanted to and not because everything you touched was unlucky and stupid.

The lights of the pool shone up through the water. Her father had pulled the cover back, like he always did for company.

Allison sat down at the edge and let her feet slide into the water. She pushed herself off from the edge and shut her eyes as the water closed around her tee shirt and her underwear and her neck. Leaning back, she took one deep breath, then floated silently as the pool covered all but the circle of her face.

One thousand one. One thousand two.

She flipped to her stomach and swam under and opened her eyes.

Tick, tick.

It occurred to her that her body was 90 percent water, and she imagined the substance of her self as an Alka-Seltzer tablet fizzing into her own liquid 90 percent. Then she saw this suspension quietly puddling outward, into the pool, until any trace of Allison was diluted beyond recognition.

Then Flip came paddling up from beyond a pocket of light. There was no blood on him anywhere; his legs pedaled in neat round circles, and his one ear flipped forward in greeting, pink tongue undulating in the water.

"Flip," thought Allison, "I'm sorry about leaving the door open. It was my fault you died."

The hamster appeared, riding Flip's back. He wore a fedora and a polka-dot bow tie.

"I'm sorry about you too, Lancelot, " Allison told him. "Don't blame Flip. I should be more careful." The hamster jumped off the dog's back, and both animals treaded serenely in front of her.

"Allison," said Flip, "it's not *your* fault."

"My dearest Allison," said the hamster in his stuffy accent, "it's stunningly clear to us—one thousand forty-eight—that none of it is *your* fault."

Fifty—and her lungs had no patience anymore. They wanted up and her whole body wanted up fast, and something was helping: a tiny humming, like the high, underwater scream of a motorboat, and a parachute of pink nylon opening on the water—her father's running shorts.

Then she was up and on the cement, the air fitting her face like GLAD Wrap and still no breath coming.

Allison. He was saying to her. Allison. Then she threw up. Water.

Allison's mother took her wet shirt and underwear off and wrapped her in a thick towel, one of the ones she reserved for overnight company. Baby Ben cried, and her mother went and got him and put him to her breast with a kitchen rag draped over his head. She sat on one side of Allison at the breakfast nook. Allison's father sat on the other. Did Allison want a glass of water? Her father wanted to know.

"Okay," Allison said quietly, though she didn't want it. He filled the glass and set it in front of it. Then he sat back down and they were one on each side of her again, looking and saying nothing.

"Quit staring at me," said Allison in a small voice, "God." Baby Ben's mewly eyes peeked out from under the tea towel and met Allison's, and he made a vowel sound, and still her mother's eyes didn't waver, and her father's eyes didn't waver.

"I'm sorry," said Allison as they watched her, but she didn't mean it. She wasn't sorry for anything. The house, warm and still, surrounded them: the clock ticking and the fan whizzing and the dishes from company dripping silently dry.

Ozzie the Burro

Dear Will,

My name is Grace. I am glad you liked my picture. Maybe there are other women who sent you
pictures and you're writing to them too. I only
chose yours. I understand either way, but please
tell me if you are writing to others. You said
'a truthful relationship is the most important
thing.' This is the most important thing to
me, too. In my life there has not been enough
of that. In fact, I'll start by saying that I'm
correcting this a lot as I go. My spelling is

poor, and I'm using the computer to help with it. I have grammar check on too but some things it marks don't make sense to me, or if it slows me down too much I start to ignore it. I did not finish high school. I am currently working on a GED equivallency. I want to be truthful about that and a few other things. I think if you like me, you'll like me whether I have high school or college or not, and any other things I might tell you here. And vice-versa (I tried to spell that *visa versa*, an example that shows you the kind of mistakes).

Anyway I hope you'll like that I'm truthful, which was why I picked you, not that I didn't like the picture. I was not picturing someone like you at first but you look like a very good, solid person and carry your weight well. I don't mean to offend you. I am not perfect and here are some things related to that.

First, I am forty. This is not young, but you said I did look young. In fact the picture I sent was maybe taken quite awhile ago, before I actually needed false teeth. Now, just recently, I got fitted for the teeth and they came in, but I didn't get them in time for the recent picture they wanted and did send an old one. Also, my hair is still long, but in the picture it was only a little gray, now it is all gray. So I will send you another picture so you can judge better. I didn't do this to lie in any way, only that I really just got the false ones, and wanted to be smiling in the picture.

You probably think forty is young for false teeth. I won't go into why I needed them, only that it wasn't related to brushing, which I do, but with not getting to the dentist when some people could of. They look pretty natural. I only got them recently, in fact, and it's because my dad died that I had enough money to get them, and this computer, that I'm writing to you on. I suppose it gave me the courage to try this Service that we're trying.

You say that you are divorced. Do you mind me asking why?

I never married. I have a son who is twenty five and does okay for himself, but still lives with me. My son has a girlfriend and she is expecting, she lives here with us for the moment. I don't have a husband, because I had my son when I was fifteen, and his father was also my father. My son is not retarded at all. He's normal.

I'm sorry if that knocks the ___ out of you. I don't like people who tell you everything at first, either. I wasn't sure if I should say it. I typed it in and deleted and then typed it in again, then finally I thought that it was something you might discover after a long time, and then say ARRGGH (no spelling available) and run in the other direction. That, or the teeth, maybe the teeth even more so. I can type pretty fast. I began typing in high school. I did stop high school when I had my son, but I always read the newspaper and a lot of books and sometimes I look things up when I read, words and things. I read Mysteries, mostly.

If you'd rather not keep e-mailing, or meet me at this point, it's okay. I just wanted to get it out on paper, though e-mail isn't paper. I

like it though. I think it let's me say what I
wanted to say.
Sincerely,
Grace

Dear Will,
Thanks for your e-mail. I'm glad that you liked
the new picture. My son scanned it for me at
his girlfriend's work. He's smart about a lot
of things. His ACT was high enough for college
but he didn't want to go right away. He worked,
and then waited a little too long and now he
has his girlfriend and so on.

You say that you're wife went behind your back.
That's a terrible thing so it's no wonder that
you don't want to rush into anything. Does this
mean you don't want to write to me anymore, or
just that you don't want to meet me right away?
When you say that the other women who you got
were "ridiculous" what do you mean? I guess
I'm happy for it, but I wonder what you think
counts as ridiculous in a woman. Yesterday after I got your letter, I saw the neighbors pull
out their driveway. I knew they'd be gone all
weekend so I went over and bounced on their
trampoline. I was bouncing and laughing like
a crazy woman. Do you think that's ridiculous?
Like I say, I'm forty, but my knees are good
and I think I could climb a tree if I wanted.
I'm pretty small in build.

When you say I SEEM to be "totally honest," I'm
glad. That's what I'm trying to be when I write
to you, but in life too. And I think I could
tell you something honestly. I wouldn't ever
cheat on somebody. I'm not saying I couldn't

have fights or differences with somebody, and I would not say I'd never break up with somebody, but I wouldn't go behind somebody's back.

I also want to say something else. You say that the man your wife cheated with was normal weight but you know those are not the reasons people really cheat. Why she did it doesn't* have anything to do with that, I bet. (*I wrote "it don't" and the checker corrected me!)

When you really love someone, they can be 300 pounds and you'll still love them. If you ARE three hundred, I don't mean that's the limit.

You don't have to say you're sorry about what happened to me. It gave me Lorney and he's the best thing that ever happened to me in a lot of ways, so I can't be sorry. I won't say it wasn't hard and I felt about as down as a person could get, many, many times. I bet it shocked you that I told you it. In some ways I thought you wouldn't write back. Maybe it was a test.

I want to say something else. Nobody else knows what I told you. There was my dad, of course, and he's dead now. Sometimes people have rumored it, but my dad early on, when I got pregnant, told everyone there was some man I was running around with and that was what people thought. Once some boys beat up Lorney and called him imbred, but I said of course it was nonsense. He wonders why his real dad wouldn't be curious about him and that's painful for him, I think. But pain isn't the worst thing. Firstly, it shows you that you can stand things. Secondly, you understand more about everyone around you. They all suffer and you see we're all the same in that way and so on. You should remember this when your divorce really hurts you.

That's enough of my story, and it's too much to vomit it all out right here. I don't want these letters to be just me, vomiting my life out. Tell me something more about you.
Sincerely,
Grace

――― ――――――

Dear Will,
Thanks for your e-mail. I don't think baseball is boring, but I don't know much about it. I don't think people here even know the White Sox. Even now all I see is Cubs hats if I notice it at all. But I know they won the World Series and that is the biggest deal in baseball. And one thing I did look at in the papers is the manager, Ozzie. I bet you like him, because he says what he thinks. When he calls for that one pitcher he puts his arms out wide to his sides and says, "Give me the fat guy!" That's pretty funny. That's no offense either since that fat guy is a real great pitcher. Lorney says he throws 96 miles an hour sometimes. Jenks, Lorne told me, is his name. Then he asked me, why was I interested in baseball, anyway. I didn't tell him anything yet. But soon maybe I will tell him about you, and I hope we can all meet each other.

About my dad dying. Yes, it was recent, just a month ago. You said you didn't know "what's appropriate to say in that circumstance," and so on. It's actually funny, if you stand back from it. I suppose they don't make cards in the store for this particular situation. I just now laughed out loud thinking how a card like that might be worded but I won't repeat it here!

I guess I felt some sadness. Things did change with my dad over the years. He started going to church after Lorney was born, and the pastor sent him to AA. In AA he had to tell everybody he was sorry for things, including me. He spent all his time writing his journal and going to meetings and calling this other drunk who was also clean and helping him. I don't know if you know AA, but all the drunks call each other. It's a good system and everything, but the apologizing is what they make you do. The apology is for the drunk, not for the other one. The other one could be a tree, standing there, or a post or something. There's something almost as selfish about someone like that, in recovery, as there is about someone falling down drunk all the time. But once he started AA my dad never came near me again. And he treated Lorney very nice, and Lorney loved him. Something you might not understand is why I didn't try to get away and live somewhere else, ever. At first I guess I didn't know any better, and then dad went to AA and Lorney got older and really loved dad like he might his own dad. Which he was.

You might have to forgive your wife. Until you do it, there is something always pinching at you. I don't remember my mom, but she went behind my dad's back and left and everything. I feel sure he never did forgive her and maybe ended up doing terrible things all going back to that. I guess everyone does terrible things. It's true that some are more terrible than others.

Something a little terrible about me is how much I have enjoyed the money that dad left behind. I do want a car and will get one soon, but my credit is not the best there is. So I got the phone set up by check and then quite a few brand new clothes, and sneakers, and my dental work, and this computer, like I told you. That has changed more than I can say. First of all, I'm writing to you! Did you know you can pay your bills right from your checking on the computer? Maybe everybody does this. I'm learning to do it. It feels good to pay them, I'll say that.

Maybe you'll think this is strange but I never dated anybody. When Lorney was small I went to our pastor for counseling. That was the one who sent dad to AA. He sat me down and told me he loved me and wanted to marry me. Then he tried something, too, but stopped when I told him to. He was about fifty. He was very angry when I said no. This will sound like I'm complaining, but I didn't have a good opinion of men in general, and all these things confused it.

I really did want to love someone. It wasn't that I didn't want to. Even when dad was really sick, and that was the last two years, I somehow couldn't do anything about it. I had Lorney for company. Well, I'm not saying this very well.

I'm glad I met you, or that I'm writing to you.

But you shouldn't say that it's sad about Lorney. He is the best thing to happen to me, though what happened before it was the worst thing. I can't have one without the other so I accept the first. He's a good boy and I've tried so hard.

I was really afraid he wouldn't turn out good, and this really gave me a lot to work on, actually. Everybody needs something to work on. All I wanted was for Lorne to turn out normal, and he did. My dream was for him to go to college, but you can't make your kids be everything for you. That's why I'm getting my own GED because I don't want to be bitter with him. He's kind and respectful to adults. And I want him to be happy for himself. I never asked if you had kids.
Sincerely,
Grace

Dear Will,
It's interesting what you say, that this pitcher, Jenks, had a drinking problem. I suppose that means Ozzie was the one who gave him a second chance in life really and it goes to show you, one minute you can be down and the next things can turn around. You can be drunk in triple A (Am I right? I don't get the numbers of A's in terms of double or triple) and then a few months later your playing in the World Series! Someone just has to give you a chance.

I'm sorry I asked if you have kids. Maybe it's too soon. As far as it goes for me, I'm almost a grandmother anyway! So I don't care about those problems. Except that I can tell it pains you. I do care about that part. But even if it was your fault, it seems to me you should never think you are a failure. And you and your wife could of worked on it, since there is always somebody who needs love. People adopt kids or they take in foster kids. My sister and brother lived in some foster homes and they still love those people who took them in. Well, my brother

does. He did well for himself and is a CERTI-FIED PUBLIC ACCOUNTANT. We don't know where my sister is and the last we knew she was out of her mind on drugs and probably on the streets too. She lives in Chicago. I'm sure it's nowhere near you're neighborhood. Here comes Lorney.
Very Truly Yours,
Grace

Dear Will,
I know what you mean about trusting people. Sometimes I felt too that I never could again. If you can't trust family or even the pastor, then why bother? I'm sure you felt that about your wife. She shouldn't of done what she done, but now you just need to find someone you CAN trust. That person won't be her, that hurts you, (something wrong with that sentence says computer oh well forget it) But all you need is one person you really can trust and it will be okay again. I don't mean romantic. It can be a friend you trust.

It's true your not young, but at our age, you can look at it either way. Something can happen all of a sudden and you get that hope again. That's the amazing thing in life, in my mind. For example, my dad died, and all the other things I talked myself out of over the years are coming back to me. I want to learn more things, I even want to travel to some places, maybe citys, and I want to love someone the real way. (I'm thinking of you when I say it, I'll be honest, but don't let it scare you off. If its not you it will be okay with me.) Any-ways, I don't think forty is old, at least not in how I feel now. People used to tell me I was pretty and that stopped (the teeth were part of it but not all of it I think) but I feel so different now, and in a good way. Forty! I still have some life left and can start something new. Sometimes I even start to laugh from it. Does it make sense? I hope it's not all the money making me feel drunk. That would be shallow!

And I hope it ain't you, bud. You might let me down. I'm just kidding around of course.

Do you like being outside? I really like it, to the point that I get depressed to come inside. I walk a lot. This started when I was young, I guess because I just wanted to be out of the house. The house was awful inside growing up and my dad didn't let us have plants because his mom kept them in Folger's cans and let the cans rust and the plants die and that gave him the idea all plants was just eyesores. So I got lots of plants now and I like it inside and out. But today there is snow on the ground, and the sun is shining, and along the river you see the reflection of the trees with all the snow on the branches. Some little birds were swimming through the water and you could see their paths perfect because the water was so still. Really, I feel like I never saw anything like this before. It's a happy day for some reason.
Sincerely,
Grace

Dear Will,
I also have a boss who is younger than me, Lorney's age. The place where I work now, Quality Metal Finishing, is good pay but not steady. Lately I have some kind of pimples on my face

because of the grease I get on my hands. I wear gloves but sometimes touch my face when I'm not paying attention.

Your boss seems like he is mad about something in life and just taking it out on you, but I'll tell you something I did with this grumpy woman I worked with and you can see if it helps. Put an extra Pop-Tarts in your bag lunch and slide it in his lunch when he's not looking. First of all, it's funny. He'll probably open his bag and then look up and say "What the Hell?" and you can have a laugh to yourself, which will help. Second, he probably will eat it, and maybe feel good in the end that someone did that. While your working, it passes the time to think about things you might put in there. I always made them packaged goods so there was no scare about poison or anything. This grumpy woman did get a little better. She would laugh to herself when she opened her lunch and shake her head. I got such a kick out of watching her eat the things. Especially hundred thousand dollar bars. When she pulled those out of her bag, she'd say "Oooh!" like she really did strike the lottery. All this sounds silly but it might actually work. And then, after work, maybe you can walk home. Sometimes that helps me. Of course I don't have a car just now, what else would I do! But if you walk, by the time you're home maybe you won't feel so mad.
Yours,
Grace

Dear Will,
Today I bought a burro. I paid a hundred and a half, but he's worth it. Did you know something,

he'll eat most anything. Lorney fed him Little Debbie cakes, but also macaroni noodles! Give him a carrot, he bites it, and the rest falls out of his mouth to the straw and he just looks at it like a dope. Give it back to him, he bites half of that and lets the rest drop like some baby that's figuring out what gravity is. He's got big gray ears with white fur inside them and a very soft mouth, but you can tell by his eyes he's not a thinker or anything. He's pretty short, just up to your hip, maybe. And he's got long, shaggy gray hair on his forehead. If you pet him there, on the brows, it's very thick and feels like lamb's wool.

What else? Oh, his back is very swayed and crooked, with a T marking. The vet said, it's the sign of the cross. A sacred burro, is what they're called. Sacred! It was another one of those times I wished I was religious, I love that name so much and wish it meant a lot of things. This reminds of something about burros in general. I always wanted a burro and my dad said "They're not good for nothing" (yes I know computer, I'm quoting my dad here) but I was just thinking what I should of said. "They're good to look at." It's enough. Not everything should be of some use. People should have use-less things, and love them, and maybe try more to love everything that way. Even their kids too, not because they made them look good by going to college. Guess what? If you come to visit me, I'll let you name the burro. Until then, I'll just call him after you. (That's a threat!)
Bye for now,
Grace

Dear Will!!!
It might sound terrible to you, but even when
dad was very sick and dying, we didn't used to
be able to open the door. Lorney fixed up the
garage as another house, and built a sort of
passage from the garage to the house out of
some old materials. Like a hall, I guess but
much colder in the winter. The garage sets to
the side of the house and behind it. It was
Lorne's first year in construction and he didn't
know much, so the passage is very lopsided. You
can pass through it, though, but not standing
up. So Lorne and Debbie stay in the garage side
now, where dad was, and I'm in the other.

When dad died I paid off most of the bills, but
for awhile before that we didn't really answer
the door, and when someone came to one door, we
crawled through the passage to the other place
and stayed there for awhile. I don't know if
you've ever been in debt. The kind where you
don't answer the door, I mean. Anyway, today
somebody drove up and I almost went to hide
from that habit . . . it was the UPS man! So,
all of this is to say that, I did get the pears
and they are so delicious. I believe you are
joking about them being for the Burro but if not
I want you to know, these pears are too good for
burros, sacred or not. Maybe you're not kidding,
but still, I'll eat them myself. I don't know if
you know it about me, but I love pears more than
maybe any other fruit. So thank you.

I like the fact that you send food and not
flowers, too. I don't know why.
Thanks again,
Grace

Dear Will,

I was surprised that you said your wife called but I'm glad you were honest about it, of course. I don't think you have to get my permission to meet with her since you never met with me! But it makes me realize that I WOULD really like to meet you. Like I say, I don't have a car at the moment but maybe you would like to come here. Or maybe you want to see what happens with your wife.

Since you asked my opinion, if your wife didn't want to adopt kids then I think you should of accepted that and not be angry. Well, I say this and I do have my own child. When you have one you love them and they grow up and then no girl they meet will ever be good enough for them. Debbie, Lorney's girlfriend, wants to be a dental hygenist. That will make money. I'll watch the baby once she's ready to train for that. I'm sure I'll enjoy that, and I can't wait to see that little baby. When I was pregnant, I almost never thought of Lorney and who he would be. Then he was born. I can't tell you what it was like. I can still remember how it felt to wake up and remember I had him. I was quite amazed.

Does it make you feel bad when I say that? I don't know the pain of wanting a child and not having one. I'm sorry you have that.

I'm glad you're walking home every day. Is it a little better? But why did you buy weights? Are you lifting them when you walk or after? It just occurred to me you might be doing it for your wife. Sometimes I think it's good that we're not meeting each other and other times I have thought, I wonder why he doesn't want to meet me? I'll just say that I would like to, when you feel like you're "ready".

I will say this too: sometimes I feel so happy that I want to cry. The pears, for example. It has to do with you, but don't get a big head, mister, that's not all there is to it. I'll be walking along and I just feel happy.

We live in what they call East Town, because it's east of the town. Isn't that clever? I have to walk alongside the highway and cross a bridge over the river to get to the Senior Center, where the GED classes are. There is one boy there who really can't spell. He makes me look like a P.H.D. He's Lorney's age, but to be honest, I don't think he'll ever read very well. He still does it out loud and so all of us in the room can tell how slow it is. Sometimes I help him a little bit, because you can tell when he gets stuck. It's the worst feeling to wait for someone to sound out a word. When Lorne was learning I almost felt irritated until the word came out, I was so anxious. Then one day he was just off and running. He was only in first grade. All of a sudden he could just do it. I had to hide my face sometimes, I was so proud of him. I didn't want him to think I didn't expect it. This is one happiness I have. I still think about Lorne reading and I feel thrilled all over again. But this young man at the Senior Center just blows out very loud and sighs and shakes his head. I know his folks. They live in the trailer park. They're two normal people, mother and father, and married still. But he probably won't ever read. Also at the Senior Center there's also a man as old as my grandpa was. I think he's retarded, but he comes every night. He smells like incontinence, and he gets pretty touchy if you get to "his" computer first, even though they have two and there's a twenty minute limit anyway. Sometimes I think some pretty dark thoughts where ,he's concerned, like Jesus Christ I'm forty years old and trapped in this smelly room every night, fighting with some Urinie old Coger (sp ok I know) just to get my goddam high school certificate!

When the class is done I walk back over the river. It's pretty at night that way, because the bridge is right downstream from the dam. East Town is the poor side but nobody from the West side gets to cross the river home at night. Coming over the bridge, and if there's a moon on the water, is very pretty, and hard to see in a car, I bet. It's cold at night but I have this CarHartt coverall that used to be my dad's, and some good work boots. I do look like a fool, but I'm practical and I don't care. There are some Mexicans who work at the restaurant who sometimes walk across at night too, and some have bikes and they laugh and joke with each other in Spanish. So we're the ones who get to see the moon.

When you come here, if you do, that's what you'll see. The house will look very small to you I bet. Remember the neighbors with the trampoline? Well, they have a tiny little yellow house, you can't imagine there is possibly more than a room in it. Maybe there isn't. It looks especially small with the big RV outside and the big trampoline in front of it. Lots of people have nicer looking cars in the driveway,

but not us. We have two cars in the driveway
but neither one works right now.

You asked if I lived on a farm, probably because
of the burro. (Still named Will!) The truth is,
it's like living in town, but the difference is
that we don't have zoning like they do on the
other side of the river. So at the end of the
block a fellow has about five cows in his backyard, some have chickens, and now I have the
burro. Most people don't have animals though,
they just keep junk in their yards like their
old cars and old fencing, tires, and sometimes
sinks or things like that. My dad said the
more junk they have the more NO TRESPASSING
signs they have. We laughed about that. My dad
could be funny sometimes, he would say he hoped
someone did trespass us, and give us a spring
cleaning. In the West side, which is the "real"
town, they would make you get rid of the junk,
but they make you get rid of the animals too.
I do like my Will. He runs right over as soon
as I open the door and talks to me and roots
around for food which he's pretty serious over.
He likes to be scratched behind the ears and
if I do that he'll put his head almost on my
shoulder so I'll have Lorney take a picture of
that and SEND AS ATTACHMENT He has these very
long whiskers sticking out from his muzzle,
like a cat or something. I didn't ever know that
burros have whiskers. Lorney gave him a pickle
and of course he ate that right up. I fed him
apples the other day, too, but I'm still saving
the pears for myself. One a day.
Sincerely,
Grace

Dear Will,
How was the meeting with your wife. (Ex-wife)

Well, I decided to be brave and invite you to my house on Saturday, since that's the day you don't work. Do you want to come? I'm looking forward to hearing from you,
Grace

Will,
I'm not sure what you mean. If it's not the right time, when will it be? I think you shouldn't of tried the service if your main goal was still to get back with your wife.
Grace

Will,
If the reason is NOT your wife, then maybe you should tell me what it IS. I thought it was "honesty all the way" with you, now I'm not so sure. Maybe later you'll want to write again. There just one thing I want to tell you. I read that Ozzie Geein (sp) called a reporter a F*%$##, witch, I wont repeat even the White Sox people are mad with him. Maybe he's not the great guy you think he is. Then again he says whats on his mind dont he, at least he dont keep things from people. Unlike some others! a mans not honst unless he says the whole of the truth that's what I believe. lets just forget it for now
Grace

Dear Will,

I'm sorry that I was a little angry at you. I do like reading your letters, and you say you like reading mine, and it's not honest to say I don't want to hear from you. I think about it everyday. Not every minute. I have a lot of other things going on. But then I said I wasn't going to write anymore and I couldn't stop thinking of writing. I'm used to it, I guess. And I feel like I want to see you. So I have to ask, is it REALLY not your wife? Don't you want to see me, and if not, why not?

Grace

Dear Will,

Don't be ridiculous. I'm sorry for what I said, but I don't even remember it. It feels like a long time ago, and I remember that I just said I wasn't EXPECTING the way you looked in your picture. That doesn't mean anything. I don't want you to lose weight. In fact, I pretty much can't stop thinking about you. It's probably too soon to say something like that, but it's blown up in my mind because you won't see me.

I love you.

I hope that's okay to say.

PS. Now they're sending Ozzie to sensitivity training. What do you think of that? I think you couldn't change him. He shouldn't of said what he said but he's not like the president and so on who just read what people tell them

to. And humans make mistakes. I guess you'll agree with me.
Grace

Dear Will,
Thank you for your letter. First I want to say that you don't have to say that you love me or that you feel like you might, just because I said it, but I appreciate it. I guess from what you say you're trying to explain why you would feel that way. It seems crazy since we've never MET each other. Maybe this is just how it happens. People just kind of know.

Maybe we can see each other soon. (? !!) It's your call.
Grace

Dear Will,
Okay, I do want to give you the directions, but I have something pretty terrible to tell you first. It's bad enough that it might change if we can go ahead with this, and you don't know how sad that makes it. I still have hope, but I know it might be foolish to even have it.

Lorney came home from work and I could hear him and Debbie fighting. Then he came over through the passage and he was crying. It seems like Debbie found all the AA papers, which I asked dad about, and he said he was putting them in a garbage bag in the dumpster. I was clear about it and he promised, and I even saw a bag I thought was it, in the dumpster, but even though they were all in the bag, a big black hefty, he didn't throw the papers out and it was something else he stuffed in the dumpster. The papers he stuffed back under some board games in the closet. I can't think why. Anyway, when Debbie moved, she brought some things in black hefty bags, and put them in that closet too, and then opened it up thinking it was her bag, and you can't really blame her, she started to read them. In there was dad's AA papers, like I said, and like I told you, he did a lot of writing out of these things. One paper said "ask forgiveness for what I did to Grace, and for my son Lorney." When Lorne came to me with that one he was just crying and sobbing. What I did was I lied. I'm not sure why I did this, but I said, "that's some mistake of Grandpa's. He only meant by it that he was like a father to you."

"Then why does he say, for what I did to Grace?"

I know what you said, Will. You have to start with the truth. This is what I tried to do with you and writing you has been one of the best things to happen to me, and I'm pretty sure I'm about to tell you something that will screw it up. I'm crying while I'm typing this. But I accept whatever happens.

But I told a story. I said, "What I did to Grace" is because your father wanted to stay with you, but grandpa made him go away, he was so mad I had you out of wedlock (I actually said "wasn't married".)

And then he gave me one of his very black looks that I hardly ever get from him, and he said, "If that's true, then what is my father's name?

And where is he? And what do you know about him?"

Well, he's asked these things before, but now he could look up any name on this computer with Google, which you probably know. Sometimes with those things you can pay for phone numbers and really find someone. So this time I felt like I had to say something. So, I gave him your name. First and last.

I know you might be angry with me. What I think will happen is that you won't ever come to see me now, because there would be a whole lie around you. That's what your wife did and that's why you hate women and now you'll hate me too.

I didn't want to mess it up. What I think I tried to do was just make up something that I wish was true, but I did it for Lorney. He really did love my dad, and I want him to have that, and not ruin it. I felt it was the right thing. I'm almost sure you won't. I understand.
Grace

Dear Will!
Take North Ave. (62) to where it meets highway 4, and that's a traffic light. Go left and then over the bridge and left on Mill, 22 is the number. Lorney's looking over my shoulder. He says just use MAP QUEST. I can't wait to see you. And Lorne is looking forward to meeting you. He wondered if I already told you you're about to be a grandfather. I know it's not Thanksgiving, but I'm going to make a turkey with dressing and cranberry. I hope you like that and I just

figured, who doesn't? And of course, let's not forget my burro, still called Will as of now. I promised you could pick the name. Lorne says why not a White Sock, which is okay if you want. I have an idea of who you could pick.
Love,
Grace

Wishbone

One Wednesday afternoon at three thirty-five, a girl hung out the school bus window as it slowed for the stop sign on Gordon's corner. She was fat, with a black, ratted nest of hair and dark lipstick. She crossed her eyes at Gordon, then made a circle with thumb and index finger and plunged a third digit in and out of this circle, as if cleaning a miniature toilet bowl. Gordon was glad that his own girls lived in town and didn't ride the bus. He wouldn't want them to associate with such a specimen.

It happened in much the same way the day after, except there were three girls instead of just one. The black hair and lipstick seemed to be the ringleader, while the second made a whinnying sound with the toilet bowl gesture. The third yelled, "I'm in love!" Gordon was missing a tooth and had no illusions that the girl was in love with him.

Gordon's ex-wife called him at the end of the same week. There was something that she had to speak with him about, she said. He hadn't heard from her in six months. Whenever they talked, he got nervous and joked too much, and this was no exception. "You want a date, Mama?" he yelled.

"Gordon," she answered gravely, "I want to meet with you. About the girls."

Gordon had been a bad husband to Vivian. They had married young, and she had not kept house like Gordon's mother. She said she loved him, but everything she neglected in the house seemed to say otherwise. He knew that times had changed, but he expected that these changes applied to a married woman who didn't love her husband enough to give up a few things for him, in order to make his life softer and easier. Why should she see this as a sacrifice? His family had farmed, and men had worked hard, and women made things clean for them, and fed them, and got them the telephone, and when the call finished, hung it up again because they understood that the body was tired at the end of a day of work. They did not mind it. Gordon's parents had died in a car accident while he was still in high school, but he could remember his father tapping his water glass with a fork when he wanted more meat. Gordon couldn't do that kind of thing with Vivian; she would just glare at him and walk away. If he complained about what she cooked, she would take his plate and throw it in the garbage. When she crossed him like this, he felt disrespected and raised his voice, and she'd yell right back, insulting him. He would not know where to put his anger then, and he even hit her once. Once was enough for Vivian. She moved out, filed for divorce, and received full custody of their twin daughters.

A few years after the divorce, Gordon was thought of around town as a natural bachelor, a man so far gone in terms of grooming you could never imagine his living with a woman. This decline had started immediately after Vivian and the girls had left. Gordon had stayed on in their old farmhouse and neglected things: he neglected to clean; he neglected to pay the phone bill; he neglected to repair the caulking on the windows, which came loose and jiggled in their frames as drafts blew from the kitchen through the living room. Gordon drank to keep warm and to keep himself company. He showed up drunk at work three times past his initial warning and lost his job. Raccoons moved from the empty barn to the attic of the farmhouse and from the attic to the top-floor bedrooms. The refrigerator stopped working and then the stove, and on many days Gordon neglected to eat much more than the jerky or candy bars he picked up at the Amoco station. He neglected to see a dentist when his gums became swollen and sore, and his front tooth became as loose as the windowpanes and fell out. The raccoons then descended to the first-floor fireplace, where their excrement dried in tiny bundles that resembled the kindling he'd neglected to split for the winter. Finally, Gordon abandoned the house and stretched out to sleep in his truck each night, where he felt cozy enough with his blanket, a bottle of aspirin, and his hunting rifle, secure on its rack behind the front seat.

As he declined, Vivian improved herself: she settled into town with the twins and went to school nights for a nursing degree. She allowed Gordon to give gifts to the twins on Christmas and on their birthday, but she told him what to buy and where each item could be found in the shopping mall forty minutes north of town. The requests were normally for clothing items with a particular brand name on the tag, and Gordon had to save for a month to afford them. When the day came, he waited in front of his house for Vivian's car, handing the boxes through the window like a drop-off of unmarked bills you might see in the movies.

"How's the world treating you?" he'd ask the twins as they took their presents.

"Okay," they'd say softly. They sat on the same side of the backseat and sometimes, though not most recently, held hands with each other as they eyed him. He tried to give Ashley's to Ashley and Bennet's to Bennet, but invariably he got them mixed up, and each handed the other her package quietly. They had fat blonde curls like china dolls you could order from a magazine, and they squinted at Gordon with their upper lips curled up toward their noses. One of them had a slight overbite, but he could not tell if she was Ashley or Bennet.

"How's school?" he'd ask.

"Okay," they'd say again, peering past his shoulder to eye a cat in the long grass at the roadside.

Then, though he never planned to, Gordon would end up joking again: "Pie aren't square, pie are round!" or "I see, said the blind man, as he picked up his hammer and saw!" and the girls would exhale and press their mouths shut with the corners turned up politely, though once he'd seen Bennet or maybe Ashley mouthing his words to herself and nodding just a little.

Gordon wished he could choose his own presents for the twins, and he wished he could see them on Halloween and on Easter. He wished he could go to their school programs and plays, but talking to people, other than the farmers he saw for coffee at the Amoco, was painful to him. At times he even wished the twins could stay with him every weekend, but this wish made him feel tired and helpless. There were two kinds of people, he told himself, people who controlled their lives and people like himself, who let life happen to them. Still, he left the electric connected in the house and the water, too, and sometimes he imagined that their family could suddenly start up again, as it used to be, the way a house springs to life in the middle of the night after a power outage.

Yet he'd made no moves in this direction until six months before Vivian's phone call. Then something unexpected began to happen. It started when he took a job hauling diseased livestock to a sale barn several hours north: animals with infection, dysentery, distemper.

On one of these runs, he hauled two ponies with pinkeye. They had large dark eyes with white lashes, and their manes were soft and waxy, like corn silk. Gordon liked to look at them and decided to keep them for a while. When he got the ponies home, Gordon had to mend the fence of his small paddock, then search the barn for his dad's old metal watering trough, which he rinsed and filled with fresh water. He bought gravel, and sand, and straw from his neighbors and layered them like a three-layer pea salad in one of the empty stalls.

Gordon put the ponies in these stalls at night and released them into the paddock at sunup. Before he left for the sale barn, he fed them two coffee cans full of grain; when he returned, he combed them and put strips of Mycatracin ointment in the lips of their eyes and trimmed and oiled their hooves. These few activities distracted him just enough so that he didn't drink quite as much, and when he didn't drink quite as much he saved a little money, with which he bought a phone for his truck. His business picked up.

When he'd saved a bit more, Gordon went to the consignment shop and bought a television, which he plugged in the family room of the deserted farmhouse. He hosed down a milk crate to sit on, because he'd long given up on the sofa. Then he swept the floor of this room and filled a bucket with warm water and Mr. Clean, dipping an old shirt in the bucket and getting down on his hands and knees to wash a circle around his crate. With this spot in place, Gordon began to watch television when he woke, and before he left for the sale barn, and even at night, sometimes, before retreating to his truck.

He liked the daytime shows best, where real people talked about real things. He watched shows with freaks and celebrities and normal people who'd lost weight or come out or recovered from all kinds of dysfunction. He watched shows with tips for fixing and entertaining and gardening and organizing. Some of it interested him and some was just silly, but the programs seemed to have hope in common: the idea that a person might decide to change in a small or large way and make some effort, and that life would respond to this effort. He felt a little ashamed to be interested in this: his parents would not have liked these shows. According to them, you were a "doer" or you weren't, and it would have embarrassed them to think it had anything to do with feelings or television. But soon he found himself getting up off the crate to take his lawn mower to a fix-it shop, then mowing the crabgrass that had poked around the edges of the foundation. While mowing, he discovered wild roses by the cellar door and decided to display them, using an old piece of cyclone fence as a trellis.

By spring's end, at the time of Vivian's unexpected phone call, Gordon had begun to entertain the idea of moving back into the house. He would work gradually, one window at a time, one cupboard at a time, one room at a time, getting what an expert called "visible results" so that he would not be overwhelmed or distracted.

He had this plan: when Vivian came for the summer drop-off, Gordon would tie the ponies in the long grass of the roadside, manes trimmed and shining in the sun. The girls would ask, Could they stay and ride them?

Some of the shows Gordon watched reunited children with their parents. The children confessed their hurt and feelings of abandonment, and the fathers or mothers confessed their feelings of guilt, and they all cried and hugged each other and promised to make a new start. There even were couples who had married, divorced, and then realized, finally, they had loved each other all along.

It was a good sign that Vivian had called three months before the birthday drop-off. Gordon wondered if she had seen the improvements in the place, driving by. Maybe she was lonely after all these years and starting to reconsider. People can change, he might tell her. A man, for example, can cook things once in a while. He can take his kids to a park, even if this man never did that sort of thing before.

Just in case, Gordon went back to the consignment shop and bought a used refrigerator. Once he got it home and went to remove the old one, he could see that there had been so many newspapers piled around the outlet that he'd simply not noticed that it had come unplugged. He left the new one in its dolly on the porch and plugged that in too, then bought a fresh gallon of whole milk for each, to make them look less lonely.

He showered before the meeting with Vivian, though the showerhead fell out of the wall as he shampooed, and the effect, because he had not completely rinsed his hair, was a little crispy. He thought if he smiled with his mouth closed he looked presentable. Before he left, he unthreaded the wild roses from the cyclone fence, wrapping them in some wet paper towels and a layer of tin foil. Then he set out for the shopping mall, forty minutes north of town.

Gordon arrived early. He sat at the food court with a view of the clock, waited five minutes, and approached the Burger King counter.

The girl who waited on him had a stud in her tongue. "Can I help you?" she asked, not looking at him.

"For a minute," he said, "I thought you were chewing something. But that's a type of jewelry, isn't it?"

"Can I help you?" she asked, again.

"Two coffees," he said. "One for me and one for my wife, who I'm not meeting until ten, but hey, your coffee can wait, right? Ha ha! Because I remember that lady sued over it, right?"

The girl left the counter and came back with two coffees.

"Or was that McDonald's," Gordon said, "where they did that?"

"Cream?" she asked flatly. She had an odd makeup on—white but nearly green under the fluorescent food court sign. When she talked her eyes rolled in her head, and her skinny body swayed as if she were seasick.

"I'm watching my girlish figure," Gordon said, but she'd already dropped a handful of creamers onto his plastic tray.

He sat drinking his coffee until ten, when Vivian was supposed to arrive. When ten came and went, he opened hers and began to sip it.

When Vivian showed up at the edge of the food court at ten thirty, Gordon was turning the empty coffee cups around and looking inside them. When he saw her, he put both cups in front of his face, then parted them. "Peekaboo!" he said. He set the cups down and put one hand on the wild roses, which were sitting on a chair beside him.

"Gordon," Vivian said, and she bowed her head primly. Her face flushed right up to her widow's peak. She usually wore sunglasses at the drop-offs, and in the light of the food court he noticed that the skin around her eyes had grown slack. She still dressed like a girl, though, in a tight striped top and white vinyl boots with little spiked heels, her stringy hair pulled back in a ponytail. She slid into the chair across from him and shook her head.

"Well," he said, smiling with only his lips, "I wasn't the late one, missyjane."

Resting her elbows on the table, Vivian made a tent over her forehead with her hands. As she spoke, she peered out at him from under it. "Some girls in the twins' class have started a rumor about you, Gordon," she said. "You and those *ponies*." She widened her eyes under the tent of her hands as if there were something behind him.

"I happen to know that these girls ride the bus. So from now on, I think you'd better stay inside when the bus comes by."

A rumor. The ponies. He couldn't find the words to ask her anything, but he felt a blanketing doom. His house would never be any place for the girls, even one weekend a month. He had no utensils that were not rusted, no mattress that had not been chewed through, no sheets. Even the shower was broken.

Just over Vivian's shoulder, the skinny girl who'd sold him the coffee was staring at him. She opened her mouth wide and stuck two fingers toward the back of her throat as if to make herself vomit. Then he recognized her. She was not the ringleader on the school bus; she was one of the others who whinnied while sticking her finger in the hole and out of the hole, in and out. "I love you," another one had yelled.

Vivian's eyes were misty. "It's just a rumor," she said. "I know it's not true."

Gordon remembered an old man who had lived in a trailer down the road from them when he was a kid. People had said the man did it with a cow. But that man had never married or had a job, and he spent his day wandering, talking or singing to himself like a crazy person. The police would find him in a ditch and drive him home.

"You're wrong," Gordon said, trying to smile. "They think the house is haunted."

"No, Gordon," said Vivian, her jaw setting. "It has to do with you."

She wouldn't listen. She always had to be right. This was how all their problems had started. A knot in his stomach, a desire to shut her up. "You got old, Vivian," he said. "You got old and ugly."

Her face fell, then rapidly righted itself; one of her eyelids began to twitch, as it did when she was ready to cry. He felt better then; the roiling in his stomach settled and his mind felt tolerant and smooth.

She stood and clutched her purse to her stomach. "The girls are embarrassed, Gordon," she said. "Think of them."

He reached for the roses under the seat and threw them at Vivian just as an old couple in matching sweat suits passed by. They stepped over the aluminum bundle, then glanced back at Gordon as they passed; the man took the woman by the arm.

Then Vivian was gone, and Gordon sat at the table feeling anxious. She had believed him. But she was not ugly to him; she was beautiful then and beautiful now. Somebody should be held accountable.

He returned to the Burger King counter. "Can I help you?" said a tall boy with acne.

"I'm waiting for the skinny girl," he said. "I want that skinny girl to wait on me."

The boy disappeared and came back with a manager. "Can we help you with something, sir?" he asked.

"A large coffee with cream," Gordon said.

He sat back at his table and looked up again toward the center of the mall, then down at the roses peeking out from the foil. They were limp and nearly colorless, like the wet paper towel they were wrapped in. He opened one creamer and poured it straight into the coffee. The cream disappeared in blackness for a moment, then shot up like a mushroom cloud. It looked like what might be going on in his stomach. He put the empty plastic container over his thumb like a thimble and then opened three more creamers, capping all digits but the pinky. The he took a swig of the coffee without stirring it. It burned his tongue, but he drank on. The stirring in his stomach lowered to his bowels.

He removed the thimbles from his digits and studied his fingernails. They were as long as a lady's but tough and yellow, like shells. The index fingernail had grown away from the nail bed and no longer touched the flesh at the tip of the finger. He pictured himself scratching the ponies, out there in the pasture as the bus went by, the shuddering of their skin as they fought off flies, the delicate squatting of their hocks as he ran his curry comb through their tails. No, the rumor didn't surprise him. He could see himself like that old man, wandering the road, muttering to himself. He wasn't far from it now.

Gordon drove home and watered the ponies, as the sun set and a waxing moon laid a milky cast on the lawn in front of his truck. His limbs felt sore and heavy and his mouth throbbed. It was a struggle to remove his jacket, to prepare his blanket, to open the glove compartment. He placed an aspirin tab to dissolve on his gum and spread his body across the front seat, pulling the blanket to his chin. When he closed his eyes, he saw Vivian crying, and he cried a little himself until he felt too worn to go on. He was nearly asleep when he heard footsteps passing by on the gravel.

He sat up slowly, then turned to lift his hunting rifle from its rack behind the seat. He rested the rifle on his lap and leaned forward. He could make out three short black figures walking through the milky lawn and up the front steps of the house. One had her nose pressed against the pane of vertical glass next to the front door. Gordon cracked the truck window.

"The flash isn't working!" said a girl's voice.

"It's too dark," said another voice. "We need a flash."

"Shh!" said a third voice, huskier than the others. "Did you see that?"

"That's a raccoon or something."

"Should we look in the barn?"

"He keeps them in the house, you said."

"The horses?"

"That's where he fucks them. He fucks them in the house."

Gordon slid the keys from the ignition, then silently opened the truck door and lowered himself to the ground. Still standing behind the truck, he lifted the rifle, took aim, and fired one shot at the base of the porch steps.

There was no doubt now, from their screaming, that they were girls. Two scurried off the porch and into the long grass of the roadside, while the one in front turned to the refrigerator, pulled open the door, and ducked behind it.

So, he had them. One of them, anyway. No matter who started this rumor, this one had been part of it.

Gordon fired again, aiming just near the base of the metal dolly. There was a howl from the tomcat that slept underneath the porch. It popped up through a hole in the wood and ran in the direction of the screaming friends.

Then two chubby hands shot up from behind the white door.

Gordon held the rifle steady at his shoulder and climbed the porch stairs. From the roadside, the engine of a car started up, and a husky gasp escaped the refrigerator.

"Looks like your friends left the party," Gordon said, advancing.

The chubby hands curled themselves around the edges of the refrigerator door, and there was a low sobbing. Gordon inserted the rifle in the door; the hands fell away and the door swung open. Even in the tiny light of the refrigerator he recognized her: the fat, sheet-white face, the black lips, the ratted nest of black hair.

"Don't rape me!" she cried. Her voice was heavy and thickened with sobs, like a record played at slow speed. "I'll just go along with it. Don't rape me."

He gestured to the stairs of the porch.

She took one step down and turned back to him. "Please," she said, "I have a credit card."

"I don't want your money," Gordon said. "I want you to walk yourself to the passenger side of that truck and get in."

He followed with his rifle at her back. When she was seated, he went around to his side and got in, balancing the nose of the rifle between his feet, running his hands around the smooth wood of the butt. He could hear her voice saying, "He fucks them in the house." For a moment, he saw his own cracked hands circling the black and white face, splitting it open like a melon against the porcelain of his sink.

"You're nasty," he said. "You know that?"

He could hear the girl's breathing as she struggled to control it. She was more of a mess than he remembered from the bus. Her tears had cut vertical furrows into the white face makeup, and the black around her eyes had pooled hideously. Underneath, you could tell she was not the kind of girl you could call pretty—by any stretch of the imagination. Most of her type weren't. He'd seen a show on it.

"Look," he said. "I know about you. You're a Goth."

He replaced the rifle in its holder behind the seat.

"You like Manson. Not Charles, but the singer." She glared at him, but he only wondered, when she did, why some girls had to be so homely, while others, like his own, had such easy beauty. Slenderness. Tiny noses and feet and hands. And this one, with shoulders like a quarterback's.

"Do you want something to drink?" he asked. "There's whole milk."

She shook her head. She'd probably been friends with all the kids when she was little, and then at some age it all broke up and they wouldn't have her anymore, and it became decided for her. Everything in life came down to this eventually. Everything broke, and the break was like a wishbone, with one side getting the better of it by far. What could you do, if you were the one with the tiny end? Pretend like you wanted it that way all along, like it was your decision.

"You're going to wash your face," he said.

"Oh, Jesus fucking Christ."

"Don't talk like that," said Gordon.

So the Goth went inside and Gordon followed, watching as she lathered Irish Spring all over her face and washed the white gunk off. "What's that crap in the tub?" she said, peering at the showerhead, which now poked up from a mound of drywall.

"Shut up and wash," said Gordon. "There's Lava if you need it."

"I don't need Lava," the Goth snipped. Her skin was blemished and sore with acne underneath the white makeup, and when she turned to face him he thought of the mite-infested cattle that hung their heads as though they knew they were missing great patches of their hides.

He shouldn't kid himself. The rumor hadn't ruined things for him. They were ruined long before then. A birthday gift and a Christmas gift and some child support payment—that was nothing like being a parent of somebody. It didn't get into any of it, the good parts or the bad parts. Guiding your children away from people like this. Or making sure they didn't turn into one. Some people didn't have that kind of help, ever.

As he drove her home, the Goth sat watching herself in the side mirror, blubbering softly.

"Those friends of yours are not such good friends," Gordon said.

"You're crazy," she sniffed. "Why should I listen to you?"

He shrugged. He could let her win; she needed it. She needed a lot of things. Friends, mostly. There were his own daughters, of course, but he couldn't just suggest that she be friends with them. How did he know what they were like? Snobs, probably. But he might do something for her. Help her save, maybe, for community college.

Before he dropped her home, he pulled in at the Amoco and bought her cigarettes and Diet Coke and a high-energy vitamin pill—all the things he imagined a girl of her age might like.

Helping

When she got home from work—she liked to call it work, not baby-sitting—Ruthie would kneel at the edge of her bed and ask God to control her anger. She did this because she knew she had sinned, but she had a curiosity about her emotions that went beyond her desire for goodness. She could have asked Him to temper the curiosity along with the anger, but she didn't. Instead she asked forgiveness in vague terms. "I've sinned in wrath," she'd say, or "I'm sorry for my thoughts."

Then she would go to the kitchen and eat whatever she could find, usually without being hungry to begin with. Sometimes this was a continuation of what she'd started eating at work, depending on how far she'd gotten: unbuttered popcorn if it was a good day, or frosting right from the can on a bad one.

She'd graduated from the state university in Baltimore last May and had spent the summer getting a tan, memorizing scripture, and working on a résumé. When September came, she went to the mall and bought a navy suit and some leather-look pumps with a low heel. She then mailed her résumé to ten places from the newspaper, receiving no response. Before she could send another round, her grandmother needed an emergency gall-bladder operation, so Ruthie postponed the job search to care for her, cooking her meals and reading to her in the afternoons on the marble stoop of her row house, while her grandmother sat just inside the screened window, close enough to hear everything. Her grandmother liked to see Ruthie get the fresh air, she said. And for her help, her grandmother let Ruthie take all the money she wanted from the roll of bills she kept in a cardboard orange juice can in the cabinet. A month went by, then two. Ruthie continued to live with her mother, and expenses were few. She began to indulge herself: watching television, making cookies and eating the dough, even reducing her scripture study to just twenty minutes a day, during which she would often become distracted and pick up a magazine.

Toward the end of the month, Ruthie tried on the suit and discovered that the skirt would no longer zip. Then nervousness set in; she couldn't pick up the paper without feeling tense and sweaty. So she stopped looking and prayed to God to let her know what he wanted from her.

It was her mother who found an ad for a "kind, patient person to care for cute child in wheelchair, sign language a plus."

"Do you mind if I call this number for you?" she asked Ruthie. She was a big woman with a smooth, low voice. She talked when she didn't have anything to say, just so she could listen to herself. If you sat next to her in church, you couldn't hear yourself sing.

"Just leave it me, why don't you?" Ruthie answered. It irritated Ruthie that her mother always went straight to the advertisement sections of the newspaper, as if the world and national news were nothing next to her own glossy little finds and bargains. "You think I can't get a job by myself?"

"I'm not saying that, dear heart," her mother said. "It says, call for details." She held up the paper and poked at it with a fat finger. "I thought I'd just ask what the details are."

"You don't think I can call by myself!" Ruthie sat up and crossed her arms over her stomach. But her mother had already retreated to the kitchen with the paper in hand.

The woman on the phone explained to Ruthie's mother that she didn't want live-in help, just someone to come during the afternoons and sometimes into the evening, if they needed to go out. Ruthie's mother replied that this situation sounded good for Ruthie; she'd always seemed to get a kick out of helping people. Ruthie could start the job tomorrow, when she returned from New York.

"New York!" Ruthie snarled, as her mother hung up the phone.

"I didn't want her to think you weren't capable of calling by yourself," her mother said, patting Ruthie's shoulder and drawing her hand back quickly, as if to avoid being bitten.

"You accepted the job!" Ruthie said. "*For me!*"

Her mother tucked the fold of her chin toward her chest, stuck out her lower lip, and batted her eyelashes.

"Are you under the impression that you're cute?" asked Ruthie.

"I'm sorry," said her mother. "You said you wanted a meaningful job."

When Ruthie got over her annoyance, she realized her mother was right. She liked helping people. She always opened doors for people in wheelchairs and looked right into their eyes and smiled at them. If she saw retarded people in the store, she'd talk to them about the weather or whatever they were buying, speaking clearly so that they could understand. She'd enjoyed reading to her grandmother and making sure that she got enough to eat. She knew she should be good to other people, but when she did these good things it was as if she *saw* herself doing them, which she could only conclude was because, in those moments, she had overcome herself and become someone better.

So Ruthie's mother went to the bookstore that night and bought a sign-language book for beginners, which Ruthie studied in her bedroom. While lying on her bed, crabbing her hand into the signs of the alphabet, she had an image of herself with the girl she was about to meet. They were in a meadow together on a sunny day, laughing, talking only with their hands yet understanding each other, and it seemed to Ruthie that beneath her own gestures were the most profound and beautiful things she'd ever felt or thought. And with this image came a warm, tingling excitement, traveling up her spine.

She'd had this same sensation at fifteen, sitting around a fire at bible camp, the sweaty skin of the other campers pressing against hers, crying because the week at camp was over but also because they nervously sensed something bigger happening, something reaching into their souls and opening them: "If you're willing to accept Jesus, light your candle. Light it for Him." She'd risen as if she were being pulled to the fire. It was the most blissful, complete emotion she'd ever experienced, although, looking back, she realized she'd felt everything deeply in high school. Nearly every happiness or sadness had seemed sharp enough to cut her in two.

The house was impressive—large and white, with a sprawling lawn and a sidewalk that swept toward twin pillars at its front entrance. Fancy, Ruthie's mother might say, and yet even that word seemed cheap and nondescript to Ruthie; it was grand, splendid, like a palace or a government building. She'd seen these houses before, on her walks from their row house in Hampden through Roland Park—mansions with dormers, porticos, pediments—but she'd rarely seen anyone come out of one. Her eyes scanned the sides of the house for a less intimidating entrance, but when she didn't find one, she entered between the columns and rang the doorbell. Maybe a uniformed servant would answer the door, she thought, but the woman who appeared wore a beige suit and small wire-framed glasses.

"You must be Ruthie," the woman said, extending her hand. "I'm Lynn Stone." The woman trembled slightly, so that she reminded Ruthie of a frightened animal, a Chihuahua, something so finely bred that it must be held close to the heart to calm its racing nerves.

"How ya doin'?" asked Ruthie, and when Lynn Stone didn't

answer, she could hear her own dumb accent and dumb nervous laugh following behind it into the silence. Lynn Stone led Ruthie down a hallway past a room full of antiques, whose entryway was roped off by a silken cord. At the end of the hall was a large white kitchen with a modern kitchen island in its center. Beside the island sat a tiny green wheelchair.

"This is a new friend, Chloe," Lynn said, hooking her index fingers together.

Ruthie put a big smile on her face and stepped in front of the wheelchair, waving.

Chloe lifted her head slowly. Her eyes trained on Ruthie's waving arm, soberly watching it go back and forth.

"Hi there," Ruthie said.

A bowl of brown mush sat on the tray in front of the wheelchair. In her crabbed hand, Chloe held a plastic utensil, a hybrid of fork and spoon. With a grunt, she dug the utensil into the mush and raised it up, but before the utensil reached her mouth, her head pitched back toward the ceiling, scraping the mush on her chin.

"She gets a little distracted when she eats," Lynn said. "But she likes you. She lets us know if she doesn't like somebody."

Ruthie knelt in front of the wheelchair and attempted the letters she'd practiced for R-U-T-H-I-E, but by the time she'd finished the T, Chloe was cocking her head to the side and groaning as she shoveled the utensil into the bowl. This time the mush dropped onto the table before the spoon reached its destination, but Chloe continued moving the utensil up and down without any food on it. A ragged-looking dog sat below the chair, catching bits of the mush as they plopped from the edge of the wheelchair tray onto the floor.

Lynn showed Ruthie the miniblender she'd have to chop Chloe's food in; she showed her the two bathrooms and the diaper pail and the tub, the way the wheelchair folded up if you wanted to take it in the car, how to fit the plastic braces around Chloe's legs after a nap or a bath. "It's important that she sit up in her wheelchair," she said. "It's essential that one lower her very slowly into the tub." Ruthie listened intently, bewildered not so much by the content of these sentences as by their architecture: "It's important that she be fed at six; I ask that her bed rail be raised before bedtime." Lynn's slender fingers splayed themselves gingerly over these objects as if they were very hot, or breakable.

As they worked their way back to the kitchen, Lynn told Ruthie the basic facts about Chloe. They had adopted her without knowing she was handicapped. She had been diagnosed with cerebral palsy when she hadn't begun to crawl. Six months later they discovered she was deaf.

"How did she learn to sign?" asked Ruthie.

Lynn paused. "She doesn't sign much yet, but we're working on it."

Ruthie felt a lump of disappointment in her throat. "Well," she chirped, "I can tell that there's a lot going on up there! She might not say it in the ordinary way, but she thinks it!" And as she spoke, her eyes filled with tears.

Ruthie turned her face from Lynn. She was ashamed of herself. Really, she was no better than her mother, who always went on about Ruthie's father and how he'd left them, unburdening herself to the clerk at the grocery store and to the UPS man: *Can you imagine? Leaving me with a three-year-old who still hadn't toilet trained!* Yet maybe Ruthie's heart had filled with compassion for Chloe, filled so quickly that her mind staggered behind; and she decided to believe this. She decided that she had been chosen. It was not for her to decide if the time was right.

It was exciting, at first, just being in such a big house. The fact that it had an elevator impressed her immensely. (If Ruthie had been handicapped, her mother never would have been able to afford an elevator.) Also, there were paintings on the wall. They weren't prints or posters but real oil paintings, maybe by real artists, though Ruthie didn't know about this sort of thing. There was a third floor that seemed to be entirely unused, though its rooms were filled with antique furniture and what Ruthie thought were Persian rugs. There was a screened sleeping porch on one end of this floor and on the other end a library with a rolling ladder and sets of books in all one color, some in French and some in English, and some in other languages that were not even written in the same letters as French or English.

On her first day of work, Ruthie was eager to use the signs she'd practiced, so she sat next to Chloe in the living room with a crate of books and selected one with drawings in sign language in the margins. BUNNY-HOP, Ruthie signed. She turned the page. BUNNY-EAT-CARROT. Chloe stared at Ruthie with her mouth open. Her teeth were too big for her head and stuck out from her gums at an unfortunate angle. BUNNY, Ruthie signed again, shifting so that Chloe might see the picture better. Chloe extended her arm, clamped the book in her hand, and let it drop on the floor. DIFFER-ENT? Ruthie signed. DIFFERENT-BOOK? But Chloe was studying her own hand with a puzzled expression on her face, as if she were noticing it for the first time. After a few minutes, she turned to Ruthie and moved her right hand in an arc. OUT? asked Ruthie. Chloe repeated the motion.

Ruthie didn't like going outside when it was cold, and she didn't like walking in general. But she felt a little tired, and a walk might help to pass the time. She had to bend Chloe's arm to poke it into her coat sleeve, after which the coat got hung up on the elbow and the arm had to be straightened out again in order to pull it through. When they got outside, Chloe let her torso fall over her lap and hung that way, watching the pavement roll by with her hair nearly brushing the ground. There wasn't much to see anyway; they passed just four houses before they reached the highway, and those were hidden by trees and hedges. Still, Ruthie continued up and down the lane, up and down again, until she felt sure that forty-five min-utes had passed or even an hour, walking and muttering to herself, *Be assured, those who are righteous will be delivered,* tightening her buttocks for five seconds and then releasing, cracking her neck, looking at her watch. They'd been out for fifteen minutes.

The days began to pass this way, Chloe never signing much more than POTTY or MORE or OUT, Ruthie fighting to keep her eyes open, leaving Chloe on the floor in her bedroom with a pile of toys and hiding on the third floor with a stack of mail-order catalogs, or in the pantry, nibbling on semisweet baking choco-late, which, she thought, was only used once in a while in most houses and so would not be missed. When Chloe began to whine or bang her head on the floor, the blood rushed to Ruthie's face and her jaw clenched, and she sensed a danger that was more interesting to her than anything else about the job. This danger was also there when she emptied Chloe's potty into the toilet. The potty was filled with pellets like the droppings of a deer or a rabbit, and it made Ruthie interested in Chloe's body in such a way that it felt almost wrong to undress her, and it was a struggle for her to avert her eyes from the naked body as she knew she should. The danger was also there when Chloe's eyes rolled back in her head and her body trembled and she began to laugh. The sound was not like ordinary, pleasant laughter, but throaty, like a seal's bark. The laughing always seemed to happen when Ruthie was straining to lift Chloe from the potty to the bathtub, or when she couldn't fit Chloe's pants down over her braces, or when Chloe's elbow refused to straighten into her coat sleeve, and so it seemed like Chloe was laughing *at* her. And there came the familiar surge in Ruthie's throat and her fists tightened. And one night—after she had bathed Chloe, dried her by laying her on the floor and shoving her pajamas around the back and over the elbows and down the arms, after she had finally put her in bed and picked her clothes up from the bathroom floor and had shaken the food off them, and after she'd splashed some white vinegar in the potty, and cleaned the mush and milk from the floor and chairs in the kitchen, and put the clothes and towels in the washer and the dryer and then folded and put them away—she finally got home and removed the tiny sum from her pants pocket and began setting her clock radio for the next morning to get up and do it over again, and the alarm button stuck. She yanked the radio out by the cord and threw it at the wall, cracking the plastic. She knew she should pray about this, but she didn't. She wasn't sorry, she thought. There was a certain energy she needed to pray, and she didn't have it. She would do it tomorrow, when she wasn't so tired.

"How much money do they make?" Ruthie asked her mother. She was lying on the rug with a bag of potato chips.

"Plenty," said her mother. "They aren't paying you what they could."

"That's not why I asked," said Ruthie, though of course, this *was* why she'd asked.

"Ask for a raise," her mother said.

Ruthie tried to imagine this.

"Do you want me to ask for you?" her mother asked.

"No! For God's sakes."

"Well, they could afford to pay you more."

"I don't care about the money," said Ruthie through her teeth.

"You're just discouraged," said her mother. "You need to find the trick in getting through to her."

Ruthie folded the top of the chip bag over and sat up slowly. "I read her books," she said. "Most kids like that."

"She's not involved enough. She's just watching." The cat jumped up on her mother's lap. "What does she like?" Her mother took a pair of scissors from the end table and started snipping at some matted fur on the cat.

"She likes the bath," said Ruthie, "but I can't keep her in there all day."

"What about swimming?" said her mother. "The Donaldsons have a crippled girl who goes down to the Rec Center," her mother said. The cat yowled and jumped down off her lap. "Oh dear," she said. "I hope I didn't cut the skin again."

Ruthie sighed. "I don't know," she said. "It seems like so much trouble."

"I'll call the Donaldsons and find out the hours, and then I'll pick up some of those inflatable things to go around her arms," her mother said. "And tell the lady she won't have to pay me back. If it helps, it's my pleasure."

Ruthie lay in bed that night thinking of bath time. She liked baths herself; she liked to submerge her head and listen to the sound of herself, humming and breathing in a way that was more than sound: she could *feel* it somehow. For Ruthie, the bath was a different world. It made her different. And when she gave Chloe a bath, she felt this transformation, too. With the weight of Chloe removed from Ruthie, with the curtain drawn to give Chloe privacy, Chloe seemed like a real person. There were only a few inches of water, but Chloe made noises to herself and laughed afterward, as if she could hear them.

At the Rec Center, Ruthie carried Chloe to the shallow end and placed her upright on the steps, where she stared at the water. "Come on," Ruthie said, fluttering her hands, SWIM, SWIM. Supporting Chloe's neck and back, Ruthie began to step back until Chloe's body floated in the water.

At the other end of the pool, some young swimmers were being timed by a coach. Their arms cut through the water, pulling their useless legs after them. They knew all the strokes: butterfly, crawl, even a version of the sidestroke. "Come on, Robby," yelled the coach. "That's twenty-three seconds, two more than last time, let's *go!*"

"Give me a break," said Robby, but he swam to the edge of the pool to try it again.

"Look, Chloe," Ruthie said, "try to float." She released her hands and Chloe jerked upward, taking in a mouthful of water. Ruthie grabbed her under the arms and pulled her up. A clear stream of mucus ran over Chloe's lip and down under her chin, and her eyes rolled back in her head as she began to cackle. "Come on, Chloe," Ruthie said, trying to imitate the coach's firm tone. "You have to float before you can swim." Her eyes scanned the edge of the pool for the diaper bag.

"Need a Kleenex?" A girl from the swimming group treaded next to them in the water. She swam to the side of the pool, where the wheelchairs were lined up at the end of a ramp, divided from the pool by a railing. The girl hoisted herself up onto this railing, and, like a gymnast, swung her body over it and into her wheelchair. Reaching under the seat, she pulled out a clear plastic bag, which she tossed to Ruthie.

"Thanks," said Ruthie, pulling a tissue from the bag. "I'm trying to teach her to float." She wiped Chloe's nose and handed the bag up to the girl.

"Gimme the used one, too," the girl said. "I'll throw it out for you."

Ruthie handed the used tissue toward the girl, who wheeled herself to a wastebasket, released the tissue, then sped back to the railing, mounted, and dropped herself back into the water. She then swam to Chloe and Ruthie and resumed treading water. Her eyes fixed sharply on Ruthie, the girl took a deliberate sip of the pool, then spit in a tight stream from one side of her mouth.

"How old is she?"

"Nine," said Ruthie. "But it's her first time swimming." She pointed to Chloe and signed SWIM.

"Is she retarded?"

"She's deaf," said Ruthie.

"I can tell *that*," said the girl. She looked at Chloe. "It won't be too easy to teach her to swim," she said flatly. She swam to the other side of Chloe to complete her inspection. Chloe cocked her head to one side and released a guttural moan. Ruthie realized in horror that this was the same sound Chloe used when she was straining to have a bowel movement.

"It's just a matter of finding a way to communicate," Ruthie said. She held Chloe at arm's length but found no sign of anything escaping the swimming suit.

"Tough," said the girl, with a low, whistling sound.

"Hey," said Ruthie, trying to sound casual, "how old are you, by the way?"

"Eight and a half," she said, smiling proudly. Her teeth were even and white.

"Oh," said Ruthie, "you sure are a good swimmer."

"I only use my arms, you know," said the girl. "I'm paralyzed from the waist." She narrowed her eyes.

"That's good," said Ruthie. "I mean, the swimming is good. The fact that you can swim."

"I know what you meant," said the girl, and she turned and swam away.

———

Ruthie went home that night, put a frozen pizza in the oven, and ate it all while the crust was still not totally thawed. When she went to bed, she had gas that was painful and foul, and she tossed and turned and blamed herself for losing control, for eating so much and lacking discipline in general. She was uncomfortable, that was why she couldn't sleep. Her fat was spilling all over the bed. She shifted the pillows so one was pressed into her bloated stomach and the other between her legs.

She should be praying, but her head was not clear enough for praying because she'd eaten so much, and she never would have eaten if not for Chloe, and she felt angry thinking of the girl in the pool who said it would be tough to teach her to swim. "Everyone is equal in Jesus!" Ruthie responded to the girl, and then she said it out loud, to make herself hear it. "Everyone is equal in Jesus!" But as she repeated it, the image of Chloe kept inserting itself into her mind—Chloe, with her big buck teeth and twisted body, her helplessness, and her empty expressionless face.

The next morning Ruthie's mother had to wake her up. Ruthie pulled on the same clothes she'd worn the day before and heard her mother in the kitchen talking on the phone: "Her alarm . . . yes . . . well, as far as I can figure, the cat was playing with the cord. When I realized what time it was I—"

She arrived twenty minutes late, and her head pounded all morning. She moved Chloe from car to wheelchair, from wheelchair to table, and back to the wheelchair. She took off her nightgown and put on her braces and clothes, then put on her bib and got her breakfast. She watched her eat cereal. She removed her clothes, which were covered with breakfast food, and took her for a walk up the lane and back again. Up the lane and back again. She put on her bib, pureed her hamburger, and when the hamburger spilled into the brim on the cupped edge of the bib, she spooned it back into the bowl so it could make the trip again. She changed Chloe's clothes again. She sat her on the potty. She emptied the pellets into the big toilet. She sat her at her play table and then in her wheelchair. She microwaved a beef-meatball dinner, pureed it, and put it in front of her.

And when dinner was finished, Ruthie wiped Chloe's face roughly, without wetting the paper towel. She then took Chloe upstairs to the bathroom, turned on the bathwater, and began to remove her clothes, when she felt her glasses fly off her face. As she bent to pick them up, Chloe's hand came toward her again, grabbing a chunk of hair. Ruthie jerked back. There was a rip in the middle of her scalp.

Ruthie slowly picked up the glasses and put them back on her face. The frames were twisted. Chloe's eyes lit up. She threw her head back and laughed.

"Bad girl!" yelled Ruthie. She clasped her hand around Chloe's arm and twisted it hard.

Chloe's lips trembled.

Don't cry, thought Ruthie. *Quit it.* Ruthie stripped the braces off one shin and then the other, pulled the turtleneck over Chloe's head, the pants and underwear over the ankles. She then grabbed the tiny wrists and pulled Chloe's arms sharply over her head, dangling her body over the tub until it was suspended over the water. She lowered the feet first into the bath, then the torso, until it was two or three inches from the water—*not enough to hurt her,* she thought—and let it drop.

Chloe's skull hit the bottom of the tub with a thud. She gasped and then let out a low whine, which rose like the sound of a teakettle.

Ruthie looked at Chloe's naked body. The stomach was puffy; the toes were purple, compressed as if they'd been bound; the legs were like a wishbone, joined by her private parts. It was disgusting, Ruthie thought; it was a joke on both of them. Her body was a useless thing, and it was Ruthie's useless job to clean it. A lack of order, of design. *Yet have this in mind, that Christ emptied himself, taking the form of a servant.*

Chloe was crying. Her face was red and her eyes screwed shut and her body was shaking, sobbing. "I hurt her," thought Ruthie, and she bent over, examining. *Okay?,* she asked her silently. How did you sign HURT? Ruthie put her hand on Chloe's head, feeling around the back, over the matted hair, checking for a bump. Chloe cried harder, twisting away and shivering. She had goose bumps, Ruthie noticed. She had to get her out of the tub. She reached in and began to lift Chloe's arms, but Chloe shrieked and twisted away. *What should I do with you, then?* She reached in for the arms again, but more crying. Something in the arm was hurt; she'd pulled something, maybe her arm or her elbow. She'd lifted her too fast. *It's imperative that she be lowered slowly; it's essential that one take care in moving.* Ruthie reached in and held Chloe around the waist, lifting her over one shoulder, where she hung heavy and limp—*Okay, Chloe, okay*—grabbed some dirty towels from the rack—*Don't cry*—and laid the body on the floor in the bedroom.

Below the head, water darkened the carpet like a bloodstain. The body looked broken, mangled. But didn't it always look like that? SORRY, she signed, but Chloe turned her head away, not looking at Ruthie. Mad at her. Pouting. One shoulder higher than the other, one hip higher, too. Red marks on the wrists and throat. The feet twisted and purple. Chloe whimpered as Ruthie dried up and down her legs and in-between them swiftly, toweling the hair and the torso, running another towel over the right and then the left shoulder. Chloe cried out.

"Your shoulder?" Ruthie said. "It's your shoulder?"

Chloe's lower lip still quivered, and fat tears began to run down her face. "Oh, don't cry, my fault, my fault," Ruthie said, and she picked her up gently, holding the body in its towels. She sat there with Chloe in her lap as she cried, patting the top of the head until Chloe's breath started deepening, and her whimpering stopped, and she'd fallen asleep.

Then Ruthie laid Chloe in bed, working the nightgown over her torso and arms and down, covering her, turning on her night-light.

She looked at Chloe sleeping and wanted to cry. *Go downstairs,* she thought, *there's nothing you can do anyway, and you're only feeling sorry for yourself and what will happen.*

What will happen? The whole house was dark, and Ruthie stood in front of the refrigerator again, eating like an animal in its tiny light, surrounded by the dark and gorgeous house, eating shit, eating crap she didn't even taste, the ragged dog running around her feet and eating crumbs as they dropped.

She wandered into the hallway, past the living room, stepping over the cord and into the forbidden room with the antiques, prowling around the coffee table, the wooden secretary, the sideboard filled with crystal. They might come in now any minute, she thought, and they'll be smiling their tight smiles and suspecting nothing and saying Hello, how's our girl?

She twisted my glasses and pulled my hair and laughed at me and I was angry and stopped being careful. I may have dropped her a little, and I thought she was hurt and I was scared, but I think she's really not hurt; she's okay. This was unacceptable. This was the truth.

Here was another: *some things can't be overcome.* Even with the help of Jesus, some things can't be overcome.

This was also unacceptable, but she knew it was true. She felt as if she could see the old Ruthie receding, as if she were watching her from the window of a moving vehicle, the lighting of the candle blurring from what they called a "personal calling" to some stupid, meaningless motion. Rising, bending, lifting, nothing.

When she got home, Ruthie walked to the sofa, fell face forward, and lay motionless. The television was on. Her mother was in the kitchen, making a vegetable tray for her walking club. "You okay?" her mother called, walking into the living room and standing over her, eating a celery stalk. "You okay, hon?" she asked again.

Ruthie propped herself up on an elbow. "Will you stop chewing your cud?" she yelled. Her mother retreated to the love seat, folding her fat legs underneath her. Then she went into the bathroom, came back, and sat next to Ruthie on the sofa, her hips squishing into Ruthie's shoulder. She puffed some baby powder under Ruthie's shirt and feathered her fingers lightly over her back in a way that made Ruthie realize she hated her mother's back rubs. They were always so light that they made you realize you needed a real back rub, from someone with strong hands, and she pressed her head into the pillow as her tears formed a wet spot under her cheek.

The phone rang.

"Don't answer it," Ruthie said, and her mother didn't ask any questions. Her mother didn't even answer the phone later, when Ruthie was standing right in front of it, in the kitchen, or when she was upstairs in her bedroom looking at catalogs. Ruthie knew that, when the time came, her mother would pick up the phone and say something to make the calls stop. That Ruthie had been in a car accident. That Ruthie's grandmother had another operation and she was needed at home. That there were no questions to answer, and Lynn Stone had better find other help. That she'd better stop calling here.